D1368056

Praise for *Teresa and the Cowboy*

Evoking a time in Tucson that is now only a faint memory, *Teresa and the Cowboy* expertly tells a romantic tale from 1891. Based on extensive historic research of the period, the novel traces the tribulations of the 37-year-old Teresa Velarde and her older suitor, Jack O'Brien.

Tucson was then, as it remains, an intermingled mixture of cultures and traditions. Among the true events woven into the fabric of the story are the Camp Grant massacre, the role the Wishing Shrine played in the community, and the bitter and ultimately deadly feud between Dr. John Handy and attorney Frank Heney.

Using these episodes along with a Tucson of long ago, Barnes has written an interesting story that is enjoyable to read.

—*David Devine*

Mary Ellen Barnes

Teresa and the Cowboy

Un Cuento de Amor Tucsonense

East Baton Rouge Parish Library

Teresa and the Cowboy: Un Cuento de Amor Tucsonense

Copyright © 2012 Mary Ellen Barnes. All rights reserved. No part of this book may be reproduced or retransmitted in any form or by any means without the written permission of the publisher.

Published by Wheatmark®
1760 East River Road, Suite 145,
Tucson, Arizona 85718 USA

Cover photo courtesy of the Arizona Historical Society/Tucson, AHS Photo Number 42013.

ISBN: 978-1-60494-692-5
LCCN: 2011936264

A little fire is quickly trodden out,
Which, being suffer'd, rivers cannot quench.

— William Shakespeare
Henry IV, Part III

The author is grateful to Mary Jo Yrun and Victor Chacon for providing the Spanish dialogue and terminology for this book. In addition, Victor shared his Sonoran family traditions that enrich the story. Special thanks to historians, Jim Turner and Ken Scoville, who checked the accuracy of passages about 1891 Tucson. I am also grateful to Jan Cleere, Dave Devine, Wayne Fulton, Jim Turner, and Joe Yukish for reading the manuscript. I greatly appreciate my children's help: Diana Freshwater supplied information about horses, David Barnes provided the service of editor Kelly Gibbs, and Denise Barnes designed the book cover. Members of St. Philip's Writing Workshop—Terry Ambrose, Victor Chacon, Wayne Fulton, Clark Lohr, Molly McKinney, Eleanor Nelson, Shirley Sikes, and Bert Steves—critiqued the entire manuscript, chapter by chapter.

To David, Denise, and Diana

Prologue ❖ 1991

In the ranch house's dark and dusty attic Rachel Benton skirted a discarded rocking chair and climbed over boxes and bundles of magazines to reach an old trunk. She had long meant to look into it, but couldn't because it was locked. Today she had brought up a hammer.

Once she pried off the lock, she unfolded layers of old clothes that smelled musty and ancient. From their style she guessed they were her grandmother's. Nestled beneath a partition she found small journals that appeared to be diaries—there were seventeen in all. Thrilled by this discovery, she scooped them up and carried them downstairs.

At her desk she flipped through one of them. The tarnished clasp no longer locked and the leather was cracked. A torn sepia photograph of her grandmother, white-haired and sober-faced, slipped from the diary's pages. Her left hand lay curled in her lap, an emerald ring on it. Rachel glanced at her own hand; she wore the same ring. She had always thought this ring had belonged to her mother.

Her grandmother, who died when Rachel was ten, had loved to tell stories. Rachel wished she had paid more attention to those tales. There were so many questions she should have asked her.

She began to read, carefully turning the yellowed pages.

1 Picnic ❖ June 7, 1891

Teresa Velarde picked up her pen to write in her diary, her fingers unsteady as she dipped the pen into the ink bottle. The events of recent weeks were almost too much for her to comprehend. And today he had proposed a picnic. Yes, yes, she would go with him. She could scarcely wait until Sunday.

> *June 7, 1891~ Today my new friend Jack O'Brien asked me to go on a picnic to Silver Lake next Sunday, but I said San Xavier Mission would be more suitable. Didn't tell him local rowdies, drunks & soiled doves have taken over Silver Lake. I know Jessie would stop me from going. Tell me it isn't proper to picnic with a gentleman without a chaperon. But I often take a ride on Sunday morning, and why couldn't it be with a gentlemen friend?*
>
> *I asked him to meet me in the patio behind the Emporium. Luis will be at mass with his family, & what I do is no business of my stepbrother's. As far as my mother knows I'm going on a picnic with Mercedes, outings she disapproves of anyway. If she finds I went with Mr. O'Brien I'll let her know she is not my keeper. Time I made that clear. Dear me, what on earth shall I wear? I can scarcely contain my excitement.*

On Sunday morning the sun reigned in a clear, cloudless sky, its heat shimmering on the Emporium's tin roof. Jack O'Brien stowed Teresa's picnic basket under the seat of the buckboard along with a jug he had brought along. Teresa was already swinging up onto the seat when he came around to give her a hand. Aware of her social blunder, she muttered, "Thank you, I don't need help—I'm used to mounting a tall horse. Mine is fifteen hands."

She felt she was prattling on like a simpleton. To cover up her embarrassment, she opened her parasol, a sudden movement that spooked the horse. It lunged forward, Teresa shouting, "Maldito! Damn animal! Whoa!" The horse headed straight for the patio wall. Veering at the last moment, the animal pounded onto the street. She grabbed the reins, swerving to avoid a dray rattling down Simpson Street.

Bellowing, Jack tore after the buckboard and vaulted onto it just as Teresa managed to rein in the wild-eyed horse. She meekly handed him the reins, rivulets of sweat running down her cheeks.

"Wait, hold these." Jack thrust the reins at her and hopped down to fetch his hat and her umbrella, both lying on the road. Returning, he grinned at her. "Well! Sure a bang-up start to our picnic. You're a ripsnorter! Managed like a mule skinner."

And swore like one, Teresa thought. She rubbed her lips, as if she could take back her curses and swallow them. "I have driven wagons before." She sank back in the seat, unpinning and straightening her hat. He must take her for an utter fool. And certainly no lady.

They bounced south along Osborn Avenue, stirring up a cloud of dust, and in turn they ate grit spun up from other carts. For about the tenth time in as many minutes, Teresa smoothed down her gabardine skirt. After much deliberation she had worn it with a pleated shirtwaist and a straw hat adorned with netting and ribbons. Then that cursed parasol! Ordinarily, she never carried one. Why was she trying to look like a fashion plate in *Godey's Lady's Book* for a picnic with a mere cowboy?

She was miserable, hot, and sweaty. Not in the least romantic. It mattered little—he'd never have anything more to do with her. Gloved hands clasped in her lap, she stared ahead, dwelling on her plight. After a failed romance when she was younger, two decades of viewing each single man she met as a potential suitor but discovering no reciprocal interest, she now plodded along like a horse with blinders, looking neither right nor left. Her mother and stepbrother often reminded her she was thirty-seven and still unmarried. She had been resigned to spinsterhood until Jack O'Brien appeared.

Teresa gradually relaxed as Jack smoothly handled the horse and chatted about ranch life. When they met others on the road, she smiled as though sitting next to a man and bound for San Xavier Mission was nothing unusual. Then in a passing buggy she recognized an Emporium customer who stared at her. Teresa imagined what she was thinking: there's that Velarde woman traipsing about with some ne'er-do-well. On a Sunday morning when she should be in church. Teresa wished she could shrink and blow away like a thistle in the wind. That busybody was certain to tell Luis. At the outskirts of town she was relieved when they turned off on Mission Road. But long before they reached the mission, Jack turned left on a track used by woodcutters and farmers that led to the West Branch of the Santa Cruz River.

"Where are we going?"

"To that big sycamore tree over there. It's hot and I'm starving. Could eat a bear, hair and all. That be a good spot for our picnic?"

"Yes, it is shady." She was torn by a dilemma: it was improper to picnic here alone, but at least they wouldn't face anyone else on the road. They would eat and hurry back to town. "This place brings back memories. I played here as a child. Good farmland in those days."

Jack drew up under the tree. This time she stayed put as he circled the buckboard to help her down. At the touch of his hand on hers, a scene that took place years earlier flooded her inner vision, and with it a taste of chocolate, a memory that sickened her.

October 17, 1879 ~ Jessie sent my new friend from Fort Lowell away last week. Corporal Charles Samuels III. He came to take me for a ride in a buckboard he rented from Leatherwood's. Jessie had me make Hot Chocolate while they talked in the parlor. I couldn't hear what they said. But his face was serious. He blew on his chocolate & got froth on his moustache. He drank it quickly and left. I cried alot for a few days. Jessie told me, Tess, it is a Blessing he is gone. Life as a soldiers wife is not a happy one. Jessie married one, but she wasn't happy with Papá. If I could marry Charles I would be so happy. I know I'll never see him again. That was surely my last chance for love. I'm 25, I'm an old maid. Thanks to my mother.

Jack hauled the picnic basket down from the wagon. "Feels mighty heavy. And I'm mighty hungry."

"I packed chicken, tamales, tortillas, and tomatoes from our garden." Teresa shook out the tablecloth and sat on its edge to unpack their lunch. Then the impropriety of picnicking in this secluded spot struck her again. Why on earth was she here by the river with a man? Well, why not? She was not a timid maiden of twenty anymore. She handed Jack a tin plate. "For dessert I baked biscochuelos, anise cookies."

"Just a minute." Jack set his plate down and fetched the jug from the buckboard. "Looks like pretty good eatin'. Here's something to wash it down with."

Teresa had forgotten about his jug. "I brought water."

"That'll do for the horse. This is good Madeira wine. Don't most ladies like wine?" Jack sat beside her, a wide smile crinkling the corners of his eyes, eyes that matched the sky.

"Sí, I suppose so." Teresa did drink wine, since her mother fancied it now and then. A feather of suspicion about Jack's motive for bringing wine drifted across Teresa's mind, but she fluffed it away.

After a second helping of food, Jack lifted the wine jug for another pull, wiping his mustache with the back of his hand. Then he removed his jacket and pillowed his head on it, stretching out on the leaf-littered ground with a groan of contentment. "Good vittles, Teresa."

"Just plain fare." She had only picked at a tamale, her appetite reduced by a butterfly stomach. A few sips of wine had gone straight to her head.

Jack was soon fast asleep.

Teresa closed her eyes, reliving his first visits to the Emporium. On his third appearance, her heart had thumped on hearing his big-barreled laugh ring out as he joked with someone on the sidewalk.

"Buenos días, Señorita Velarde," Jack said as he removed his sweat-stained hat.

"Buenos días, Señor O'Brien, may I help you?"

"Well, you may call me Jack, señorita. And with your permission, may I ask your name?"

"Sí, you may ask," Teresa replied.

"¿Sí?" His thick eyebrows had arched in surprise.

"Claro. You *may* ask, and I *may* tell you my name." Then she smiled and he obliged her with more laughter than her jest warranted. "Pues supongo, I guess my name is Teresa."

"You guess? ¿Que no sabes?"

"Sometimes I'm called Tess." She toyed with the rawhide shoe-laces on the counter.

"Pero prefiero Teresa. Such a beautiful name."

"Gracias, señor." She noted that his Spanish was pure, though his English was not. The tongue of her beloved father and Tía Socorro, Spanish was the language of love to Teresa.

At that moment Luis had strode in the front door. At the sight of Jack he narrowed his black eyes, looking as if he wanted to punch him in the nose. Thin and wiry, her stepbrother was no match for the bulky cowman. "My sister has work to do. Anything you want, Mr. O'Brien, I'll see to it."

"Nothing today, gracias. Just passing by, señor."

Unwilling to cause a scene, Teresa retreated to her office. Her hand on the doorknob, she stiffened, turned, and glared at Luis, feeling like a hen ruffling her feathers to guard her nest. "Good day, Mr. O'Brien," she said defiantly. "Please call again, anytime."

Teresa opened her eyes. Jack was still asleep. Lightheaded from the wine and uneasy about sitting beside a sleeping man, she decided to walk along the riverbank.

Everything looked different when she had come here as a child. Mesquite bosques then defined the river, a swath of green snaking through the valley. In the rainy season the river flooded its banks to become a shallow lake spread over wide grassy plains. But over the years, water had cut the channel deeper. Now the river's flow was reduced until the summer rains came. Teresa heard that the change came about from herds of cattle tramping the ground and farmers building ditches and digging wells.

She sat on a rock idly watching the water, now little more than a trickle. She whispered: "River, you've grown old. I remember your childhood—mesquite, cottonwoods, tules growing in green mossy bogs, horsetails to blow through, turtles in golden grass, and speckled fish darting in your clear water. I too was that young River, I too a child. . . Now I am older, barren, useless. . . Or will summer floods come rushing into my life and revive me?"

Nearby, a sparrow tussled with a broken blade of grass. Finally balancing it in its beak, the bird flew up, only to drop it. Teresa scarcely blinked or breathed, watching the determined sparrow grasp it again and wing away, trailing the long stem behind. Ah, success this time. Then she noticed that an ant had taken up a similar task, towing a dead bee around a log.

Teresa spoke aloud. "Rounding the Straits of Hormuz, little Ant? Where did I read of such a place? *The Travels of Marco Polo?* I'll go with you, Ant, to visit Xanadu, to meet Kubla Khan and his stately pleasure dome. I'll crawl, walk, or fly with you, my tenacious friends, Ant and Bird. No, go on without me. I have Jack. Ah, Jack, a suitor at last."

Decaying mesquite leaves gave off a dry sharp smell. She stared at the warp of green and the woof of dark mesquite branches above her. Long threads of silent sun filtered through the canopy and interwove with grasses, fallen leaves, and brown pods at her feet. Teresa, transposing the two tapestries, seemed to float up. Suspended among the branches, she looked down to her heaven. Her heaven was sitting in a bosque not far from a suitor she had picnicked with. How fortunate she was to dwell in a sphere with twin heavens.

Teresa came down to earth and began to tremble. I was seen in a wagon with a man without a chaperon. All Tucson may learn of it, and I know what they will surmise. Well, let them think what they will. I will not be shackled by convention. At last I am courted. The devil take all of you who would deny me that! You, Jessie, most of all. But I can face your fury if I must. And I hope that I will soon have reason to leave you for a home of my own.

A branch snapped, footsteps crunched leaves. Her automatic response of terror was unreasonable—the Apaches had been recently contained. But it was Jack, carrying the wine jug, who parted mesquite branches. "Wondered where you gallivanted off to."

"How you startled me!" Teresa stood. The purposeful look on Jack's face caused a frisson of fear. She began to walk along the river bank. "You were asleep, so I took a stroll. Looking for something. Come. I think it's down this way."

His hand on her elbow, Jack guided her as they tramped through grass, skirting the soft ground of a cienega. "What are you looking for?" he asked.

"An old sycamore. A wonderful tree that fell across the river, but it still grew. I guess it's gone now. So many of the trees have washed away in the floods the past few years."

"Let's keep looking then. OK by me. Still some good timber here. You say you used to play in this bosque?"

"When I was five or six, Lito brought Luis and me down here. Lito's a Yaqui Indian, worked for my father. He raised corn and beans and squash here. We came only a few times. Then the Apaches flared up again."

"Cussed Apaches! Tangled with them myself in Sonora," Jack said.

Memories drifted across Teresa's mind.

My diary The Year is 1861 the month is July ~ Papá and Jesie have been fiteing. She was mad cause Papá let Lito take me and Luis to the fields. Jessie said he was crazy the Apaches mite kill us Papá said they were good all spring But Jessie made him say he never wood do it again. Papá said she never liked anything he did he went off and staid out all nite. she was boiling mad wen he got home she said he stunk of the gutter I hate it when they fite.

"Just why are you looking for this tree?" Jack was asking her.

"Here it is! It's still alive, but not nearly as big as I thought. Luis and I played on it. It was a pirate ship, and we did deeds of derring-do. I ran across it without a thought then."

"Pretty brave. Reckon you still are. Just like this morning, you handling that horse without quaking in your boots like some silly female." He gave her an admiring glance, and his look awakened her from head to toe. Certain she was blushing, she turned to face the river.

"Let's sit for a spell. Cool and shady here." Sitting on the rooted end of the nearly horizontal tree trunk that spanned the river, he lifted up the jug. "Más vino, señorita?"

"No gracias, señor. I've had enough."

"One little sip won't hurt. Teresa, sit down. Hablaremos. Por favor, let's talk." He took off his hat, snatched her hand and gave a playful tug. "I know you are a proper lady. No mas quiero conocerla un poquito mejor. No, I want to know you a *lot* better. Anything wrong with that?"

"Nada, Jack, nada." She sat and smoothed her skirt over her knees with one hand, staring at the work-callused hand wrapped around hers. Qualms at being alone with a man in a secluded bosque danced through her mind again. She should walk back to the wagon—no, she should run. But she couldn't move, seemingly as rooted as the dark-trunked mesquites around them. He offered her the jug again, and she tipped it up to her lips. A smile deepened the crow's feet at the corners of his eyes—eyes that appraised her frankly. He unpinned her straw hat, placing it on the log before he slipped his arm around her waist. Tilting up her face, he pressed his lips to hers, his mustache brushing her cheek.

Teresa had waited a lifetime for this kiss—her corporal's peck on her cheek nothing compared to this. Her heartbeat pounded in her ears, from both fright and anticipation. Dios mío, she thought, I will not run from this moment. I want Jack's arms around me, his lips on mine. Laughing softly, she raised her face again. His kiss became insistent and his free hand began to rove. She pushed him back, her resolve to acquiesce flitting away.

"¿Qué pasa, querida?" Jack asked.

"I—I don't know you well enough for such liberties."

"You are a grown woman, decide for yourself. Teresa, eres muy linda. Such pretty eyes. Green fire." He lightly kissed each eyelid. "Te amo, Teresa."

The notion that she was a jackrabbit pursued by a coyote flashed through her mind. His sudden profession of love was pleasant to hear, but it still jarred her. Love doesn't blossom so quickly. Perhaps it was simply something he thought she wanted to hear, something that suited his purpose. It suits me too, she thought, I want to be loved. Can this be Teresa Velarde, the discarded old maid trysting in a mesquite bosque? Her ebullience bubbled up in a giggle. "We should go back now." She stood up.

In silence they walked back, repacked the picnic basket and stowed it in the buckboard. When Teresa walked round to climb onto it, she waited for Jack. He pulled her close and tenderly kissed her before handing her up. Silent on the drive back to Tucson, she found her mind flitting between exhilaration and shock. She was as tremulous and unsteady as a newborn kitten.

Jack was also in a thoughtful mood as they headed back. This one! She's different. For a big strapping gal of her years, she's sure a babe in the woods. Seems savvy in so many ways, but not about men.

When he had first met Teresa Velarde, he was looking around for a certain woman that Ned asked him to locate. He doubted if Teresa was the one, and he should move on. Yet, something about her attracted him. She was strong, capable, and a lady—things he admired. If not strictly a beauty, she was handsome with her dark hair and green eyes. For sure she's a green broke filly. Green broke at her age.

Teresa might be the one to put an end to his wandering. Someone to cook meals and take care of him when he was an old fogy. Marrying and settling down was a possibility that he was about ready to consider. For God's sake, he was fifty-four. But before he was hobbled, he had to strike the mother lode one way or another. He'd like to own a little spread of his own before he got hitched up with a wife.

Money! Always came back to that. Rotten luck he never found a gold strike worth a fortune like Ned did. Damn, he'd never saved his wages either. Always seemed to run through his fingers like water had run through his empty rocker in his placer mining days. How long was he gonna go on in life always sucking the hind teat? Well, he was holding down a good job at Dos Colinas. Now, if only he could just get shut of that itchy foot that made him pull up stakes after a few months on a job. He also needed to walk away from them gambling tables. He'd lost his stack of chips to the "bank" too many times. If he'd cut out gambling, he might put some money away. Yes siree, he thought, I'm gonna turn over a new leaf, quit gambling and save money. . . Hell, how many times have I promised myself that? I could damn near fill a goddamned book with all them new leaves.

2 The Emporium ❖ June 8

Teresa unlocked and pushed open the Emporium's heavy wooden door. It juddered and scraped along its crescent scar on the wooden floor. In the cubbyhole that served as her office, she sat at the desk and reached down with an old rag to wipe off her high-top shoes, accustomed to removing a layer of Tucson's dirt from them each morning. Every fiber of her being still overpowered by the memory of yesterday's picnic, she wondered how she'd wrestle with columns of figures in her ledgers. How on earth would she get through the day?

Through the open door of her office a new hat displayed on a stand caught her eye. Though loath to try it on in front of her step-brother when it first arrived, she now slipped out and lifted the hat to her head, swiveling the tall cheval mirror for a better view. She stroked the black ostrich feather cascading over the brim of the moss green hat adorned with ruched silk and netting. She might wear such a beautiful hat at Carrillo's Gardens, where Tucson's gentry met for hot baths, dancing, boating, and Sunday concerts. She drifted into wistful fancy. . . *She is wearing the hat, her fingers languidly trailing in water as Jack rows the boat across the lake.* . . Boat rides with this bowlegged vaquero? How absurd! She made a wry face and lifted her arms to remove the hat.

"No, no, wait, Teresita. Esperate. You don't wear it that way," a lilting voice chimed out. Standing on tiptoe, Mercedes Mendes lifted gloved hands to tilt the hat. "Now *that's* stylish. You look pretty today. More alive. What's new with you? ¿Qué te pasa, Teresita?"

"Nada," Teresa yearned to speak of her romance, but she knew Luis would come charging into the store at any moment. "I don't need to be stylish to keep books. Besides, I'm not pretty. I'm big and plain. Chin like a cowcatcher."

"You have good features—your dark hair, your wide cheekbones, your green eyes. You are tall and noble, like a saguaro."

"I'm a saguaro?" And with all the bulk of a saguaro, she added to herself. In the mirror she compared her own solid image with her friend's slender figure. A skilled seamstress, Mercedes made her living with her needle and thread. Today she wore a stylish blue gown she had made herself.

"Tía Socorro also compares me to a saguaro," Teresa went on. "You know how the palo verde shelters the seedling cactus. As it grows tall, the tree is stunted. She jokes about it—she's a short palo verde tree, short because I grew so tall."

"You know how the saguaro gets its start. A bird enjoys the saguaro fruits, sits in a palo verde, and after a while it plants those saguaro seeds." Mercedes's eyes sparkled with mischief.

Teresa placed the hat on its stand. "Tal cumplido. What a compliment. . . Mercedes, that new linen you wanted has come in." She pulled a bolt of cloth from the shelf, hoping her friend would quickly complete her business and leave. She planned to visit Mercedes that evening to confide in her, and tonight couldn't come soon enough.

Mercedes fingered the fabric, puckering her lips. "Sí, está bien. Cut me enough for a petticoat, por favor. I'm making it for one of my customers." She tapped the glass-topped case displaying lace, ribbons, and buttons. "And four yards of this narrow lace. No, make it five, por favor."

Teresa rolled out the fabric and began to cut it. "You missed the concert at Carrillo's last week."

"Sí. Mama and I took a drive to Cañon Sabino. Saguaros are blooming now. Remember our trips with Sister Máxima to sketch them? She called them 'las doncellas del encanto.' "

"Yes, virgins of enchantment. They are when they wear their flowery white hats. But in those days we seldom drove out as far as Sabino. ¡Los Apaches! Thank God they are at last contained."

"Almost," Mercedes corrected her. "Acuérdate, remember those savages killed a freight driver just a few weeks ago. Only a day's ride east of Tucson. The army shouldn't have pulled out of Fort Lowell in January. Too many of those murderous Apaches still around."

Teresa had read the newspaper account in *The Star* about the 'fiendish Apaches' who murdered the freighter. Although the feared warrior, Geronimo, had been captured five years earlier, renegade Apaches sometimes attacked lone travelers.

"It could have been the Apache Kid. He murders people for their horses and guns," Mercedes said. The Apache Kid, an esteemed Indian Scout in the U.S. Army, through mischance had fallen on the wrong side of the law.

"You've heard too many stories about him, Mercedes. It could have been any Indian who broke out of the San Carlos Reservation."

"Why do you defend those savages? They murdered your father and my uncle."

"I'm not, but not all Apaches want to make war." Teresa wrapped the fabric and lace in brown paper, tying it with a string.

"At heart, they all do. Some just don't have the chance." Mercedes paid for her purchase. "Adiós, Teresa, I must go."

"May I come see you tonight?"

"Claro. Of course, stop by, mí amiga." Mercedes flounced out of the store.

They had been friends since their school days, Teresa mused. At St. Joseph's Academy for Females, teachers had said that the two girls could not have provided greater contrast—one tall, gawky and shy; the other, petite, vivacious—"quick as a hummingbird," one said of Mercedes. Like her mother, she had become a seamstress. Some Tucsonans found it strange that the two girls had remained best friends after their school days. Aside from her aunt, Mercedes was her only true friend.

The store quiet for the moment, Teresa returned to the office and opened her diary. Keeping a journal had been a response to an inner need to add depth and definition to her life, an outgrowth like that of a tenacious seedling finding nurture in a crack on bare rock. Before she wrote in her journal she turned to the previous month's entries.

May 2, 1891 ~ Mr. Jack O'Brien came into the Emporium today. Didn't buy anything, just wanted to talk. He's foreman at a ranch south of Tucson. He's in town looking for a long lost niece. He is so friendly. Best beware! I thought I banished these appetites years ago.

May 9, 1891 ~ Mr. O'Brien came to the store again. He was born in Missoura. He drove for the Butterfield Line, fought in the War Between the States, turned his hand at mining & ranching. He is 50 or so, is a few inches taller than I, has a pleasant face, even features, graying hair and blond moustache and redish complection from working in the sun I suspect. I hope he will return.

Teresa hid the diary and opened her ledger, just as Luis called out a greeting. He went straight to the Emporium's stockroom to finish unpacking the new goods from St. Louis. Distracted, reluctant to settle down to her books, Teresa fidgeted with her pen. A strange notion shimmered on the horizon of her mind like a luminous rainbow.

On her walk to the Emporium the sun had burst over the eastern edge of the Santa Catalina Mountains, as two quails and a dozen chicks, scarcely larger than her thumb, skittered across the road. An impulse to follow them had seized her, to escape into the desert, into the sun's slanting rays as they painted cholla blossoms with gold and ocotillo with flame.

Escape! Was that now possible? Were not Jack and escape one and the same thing?

Escape! The word ran through her brain with the insistence and monotony of Luis's tuneless snippets of song she heard. Her stepbrother's whistling was merely a nervous habit. Serious and hard working, he donned a pleasant smile only for customers or his children.

Escape from this windowless cell. Since she was eighteen, she had bent over ledgers at this desk keeping books for her stepbrother. He had taken her out of school before graduation.

April 30, 1871 ~ Didn't go to school again today. Mercedes told me they prayed for my father's soul. I can't stop crying for Papá. Why did he have to go on that raid? Why did the Apaches kill him? Did God forget to watch over him? Sister Monica sent me a little basket of cinnamon cakes. Mercedes and I ate them all.

May 3, 1871 ~ Luis told me I wasn't going back to school. There's no more money, he said. I must work at the store. I screamed at him, I'm going to school, I'm at the top of my class. He didn't listen. He's no brother to me. He's a statue of cold stone. How could he do this? Papá was always proud of my good marks, but Luis is jealous because he quit school when he was only 14. Jessie sides with him. They never agreed on anything before, but now they're against me.

The day heated up. At noon Teresa sat on the rough bench behind the Emporium to eat cold tamales garnished with onions and tomatoes from the family garden. The old mesquite tree above the tin-roofed porch shaded the patio but offered no respite from the heat. From the clay olla hanging from a porch beam she dipped cool water with a gourd dipper. Like the dampness on the outside of the olla, her strange mood still lingered—a sense of dissatisfaction, a longing for freedom.

A whirring of wings, a raucous cry above. She gazed up into mesquite branches overhead as a cactus wren took wing. If only she could fly away like the wren, fly from the tyranny of bills, ink, receipts, musty ledgers, columns of figures, cramped fingers, cramped mind. Well, she can't fly, but she can run. Run out the Emporium door. When had it shut upon her so finally?

The desert child within her had known the taste of freedom when she ran barefooted into the desert, into the face of the golden sun—searing sand under dusty, leathery feet, freedom's cost. Running from mesquite tree shade to barrel cactus shadow to dark fence post stripe, refuges for blistering feet. Or hopping on one foot to pull out a devil's head thorn in the other. Fashioning cornhusk dolls for her younger sister, Margarita, in the shade of a mesquite tree. A forbidden dip in the acequia to cool off, splashing in the muddy water of the irrigation ditch. "Ladies don't do that," Jessie had told her as she switched Teresa's bare legs—that was the price of liberty. That child lived and breathed unfettered, basking in precious independence, jeweled moments encrusting daylight hours.

But now I am a slave—worse, an aging spinster chained to this prison cell, she grumbled to herself. And with only a pittance of a salary for clothing! Luis gives me food and a roof over my head instead, as he always reminds me. Now couldn't Jack provide these things? I dare not think such a thought. Didn't I learn my lesson with the soldier from Fort Lowell?

Teresa could scarcely wait for her workday to end. She must unburden herself to Mercedes; she felt like a saguaro with too much rainwater inside. By late afternoon the blurry figures in the maroon ledger defied her. She closed it and sat idly fidgeting with a pencil, scratching mosquito bites—mementoes of the picnic—through her lisle stockings. She thanked God that Luis was there to wait on customers; she simply couldn't face anyone and make polite conversation.

3 Convent Street ❖ June 8

Teresa walked along Convent Street. A mule-drawn cart with a large tank on it slowly bumped along the street, spraying water to lay dust. A pack of yapping dogs scampered after a bicyclist. Children played tag, darting among the few young trees struggling to grow on the rock-lined sidewalk, ignoring the horse manure, flies, spittle, and cigar butts. Adobe row houses cast long uneven shadows across the wagon-rutted road. A young man rolled a cigarette, one booted foot cocked back on the wall of an adobe house. Old women in dark rebozos sat in wooden chairs outside their front doors to enjoy the cooler evening. They called out, "Buenas tardes. Good evening, Teresa."

"Buenas tardes, señora," Teresa answered softly to each as she hurried past.

"Tamales calientes. Tamaleees." Señora Aurelia in her burro-drawn carreta overtook her. The old woman lightly handled the reins with one hand, the other steadied the burlap-wrapped kettle beside her on the cart bench. The burro drawing the cart, familiar with the routine, automatically stopped as a customer approached.

Teresa bought a dozen tamales. Neither Mercedes nor her mother was at home, but the door was unlocked. Teresa stepped in and immediately smelled cooking beans. She placed the tamales in the stove's warming oven and absentmindedly stirred the bean pot. Then she settled in a chair by the parlor's single window to wait. Outside, twilight fell.

She lacked the tranquility to determine her true feelings for Jack. When she reminisced about the picnic, her thoughts fluttered like a disturbed flock of doves. Remembering Jack's touch, his kisses, the expression in his eyes that she interpreted as love, she was ecstatic. But the impropriety of picnicking with him without a chaperon, dismayed her. And recalling his words of love, she was dubious about his sincerity. Love, built upon respect and consideration, grew gradually. But perhaps all would be well, and their love would grow like the white blossom of the saguaro that matured into red fruit.

Making an effort to brake the futile merry-go-round of the thoughts that had raced through her mind all day, Teresa fingered the starched white doily under the coal oil lamp on the table. Mercedes, like most in the barrio, couldn't afford gaslights when they became available a few years earlier. She insisted she preferred the soft glow of her coal oil lamps. As neat in keeping her house as she was in her attire, she cleaned their blackened chimneys, sprinkled water and swept the earthen floors of her three rooms. She boasted that her newest lamp came from Paris. Teresa thought the story had holes in it like those in her deshilado, the drawn-thread work in the pillowcases she made.

The front door burst open. "¡Hola! Buenas tardes, Teresita. You're in time for supper. My mother has gone to visit her sister." After Mercedes placed her basket of vegetables in the kitchen alcove, she came back and lit the lamp. "Why are you sitting here in the dusk?"

Teresa felt as if an over-wound spring had suddenly broken inside her. She burst into tears, her face in her hands. "Ah, Mercedes, if you only knew."

"If I only knew what? ¿Qué te pasa?" Mercedes sat in the opposite chair and reached across the table to take both Teresa's hands in hers.

"I haven't told you about him," Teresa began, freeing one hand to fumble in her drawstring purse for a handkerchief.

"Him? No, indeed, you have not. ¿Que hay un hombre en tu vida?" Mercedes smiled and squeezed Teresa's hand.

"Yes, a Mr. Jack O'Brien. He's been much on my mind of late, that is his visits were—oh, I don't know how to tell you."

"Ven, díme mas. Please tell me more. This Jack you speak of, has he been visiting you? At home?"

"No, he comes to the store. I haven't told you about him because—well, I wasn't sure what to think of his visits. Then yesterday we went for a drive—I mean, a picnic. To San Xavier—at least we started to go there." Teresa looked down and fidgeted with the doily under the lamp. "We ate our picnic by the river, then—well, he—¡Por Dios! Mercedes, it was so improper."

"Teresita, it's as simple as a fairy tale. You went for a drive with him, you picnicked, he kissed you, and. . ." Mercedes paused, smiling and squeezing her friend's hands.

"¿Dios mio, como te enteraste de eso? How did you know about that? Just by looking at me? Mercedes, there was no 'and' about it. There was nothing more than a kiss."

"So, there's a man in your life. ¿El primero, que no? The very first, right? Wonderful!"

"Wonderful?" Teresa spat out the word as if it were a bad taste. "Wonderful that I was alone with a man in a bosque?"

"No, the wonderful part is that he courted you." Mercedes nodded sagely.

"¿A mi edad?" Her words came out in a hoarse croak.

"Yes, especially at your age." Her carefully plucked eyebrows rose.

For a moment Teresa stared into her friend's eyes, held by her determined gleam. Something within her softened like the desert after a soaking rain. A little worm of pride wiggled up, and she smiled back. "Yes, yes it was exciting. I enjoyed his kisses."

"Mi estimada amiga, so you are in love." Mercedes stood. "I must see to supper, but we can still talk."

"What can I do to help you?" Teresa rose and joined her friend.

Mercedes puckered her lips and blew on a spoonful of beans. From a curtained shelf she handed Teresa a pot and dipped in a little water from a covered pail on the table. "They're done. Would you peel the carrots for me? I must fetch water." She took the pail, heading for the well in back that served several families on the street.

"Yo voy por la agua."

"No, gracias. I'll just be a moment or two."

Teresa peeled the carrots and put them on to cook. As she stirred the beans, a scene came to mind: María bending to stir a kettle of beans on an open fire beside Lito's hut, a jacál with vertical poles lashed together and filled with adobe. Lito and his sons plodding through dusty rows of corn along the acqueia near the Convento, chopping out weeds with hoes. He had long been a servant of the

Velarde family. She thought, beans have such a good smell, comforting.

1865 is the year. March 12 is the day I am writing this. ~ At Lito's house Luis and me, we were playing RattleSnakes. He made up a game the corral is full of rattlesnakes. if we fall off we are bitten and Die. we walk around on the bottom rail and hold on to the top rail. Luis poked me with a stick I went faster and faster until I fell off I woke up on Lito's bed. Maria scolded Luis. she gave me a Sugarcane to suck. Lito asked me how I felt and I told him about the game. then he told me a Yaqui story about a boy who dreamed a snake folowed him around the snake turned into a flute and the boy became a flute player. Lito sed snakes didnt want to harm me, but I should go round them on the trail. He said to be afraid of a snake you can see is not a bad thing, but do not be afraid of those here. He touched me on the forehead. Lito took me home Jessie gave me a dose of cod liver oil.

"Mercedes, I came here so excited by my news, I was nearly bursting," Teresa said after the supper dishes were cleared away. "But I'm still worried about what people will think."

"So this is the first romance in your life?"

"No, there was another. A soldier from Fort Lowell. That romance never blossomed."

"I think I remember him. What happened to him? ¿Y que pasó con ese tipo?"

"When he came calling at the house, Jessie sent him packing. He was probably relieved to be shut of me; I was tongue-tied around him. And I was never linda like you."

"Oh, Teresa! You could be pretty if only you would let yourself go, be free. You have always held back, so stiff and proper, so able to do for yourself. But maybe this caballero likes your independence. Maybe he is the right man for you."

Teresa sighed and fidgeted with the doily again; her fingers had removed nearly all its starch.

"If you want to marry him, you must hold back. You merely whetted his appetite with a taste. You must let him come to the table and beg. Then tell him you invited him to the bargaining table, not the supper table."

Teresa laughed. "Mercedes, why didn't you marry again?" Mercedes's husband, Ernesto, had been killed in a barroom brawl at the age of nineteen.

"I could have married again; I was asked several times, but I decided to take care of Mamá and help her with her sewing. We've always had so many good customers. Besides, why become a fat sow with a litter of piglets pulling at me? I must be the guest at the banquet, not the banquet!"

Mercedes pulled Teresa to her feet. They waltzed around the room, their skirts swirling. They bumped the table, and Teresa barely caught the tottering lamp before it crashed to the floor. Both giggled like schoolgirls before they flopped down on chairs to catch their breath. Mercedes winked at her friend. "I will teach you to dance yet, mi amiga."

4 Maiden Lane ❖ June 19

Jack drove a wagon to Tucson for supplies for the ranch. Planning to shop the next day, he left it and the horses at Colton's Corral. That afternoon as he sauntered up Meyer Street, buggies and wagons churned up dust clouds. It's hot and my throat is parched, he thought. Guess I'll leg it on up to Congress Hall Saloon for a snort or two and see what's going on in town. Sit in on a game of faro or poker after supper. Better take it easy though. Payday's a ways off.

This job at Dos Colinas pays better than most things I've tried my hand at, and life has panned out pretty damn good lately, he thought. I didn't have such a great start as a young shaver though, growing up as the youngest of nine children in a coal-mining town in West Virginia. By the time I was twelve I'd followed Pappy and my brothers into the mines as a coal breaker. For ten backbreaking hours a day I crouched over a chute to toss out rock in the coal as it rushed to the washer. Earned sixty cents. Finally decided I'd see what was on top of the earth, not just the inside of a dark hole in the ground. Ran away from home on my fourteenth birthday.

Always drifting west, I turned my hand at anything to keep my belly full. In Texas I learned to ride, in Arizona Territory to drive a stagecoach. By the time I was sixteen, if I had extra money in my pocket, I'd play a few hands of poker and down a few shots of redeye. Near the border I met Eduardo Harrington. Me and Ned got to be closer than two fleas on a dog. We drifted to Mexico, punching cattle, ending up working in a gold mine. While this hombre gambled his paycheck away in games of faro and monte, mi amigo saved his and bought land. One day Ned had himself a nice little spread near Magdalena, Sonora.

Me, I had nothing. Ned and me parted company for a bit, and that's when my luck and money ran out—even lost my horse in a game of poker. Ned's ranch was going to town, so I went to work for him. It was a good life. Hard work, no question, but not all work. My pal loved the señoritas, just as I did, and neither of us had any notion of getting hitched up. Too bad Ned had to go and die on me. Sure miss him. Well, he's gone now, God bless him. All I have left to remind me of Ned, is his saddle and his favorite horse.

Too bad I'm not aboard a horse now. I reckon it's not a far piece from here to Congress Street, maybe a quarter of a mile on top of a horse. On foot, it seems like ten. Should've stopped by to see Teresa Velarde at the Emporium, but now I've passed it. Got to keep that gal in my corral, if she don't turn out to be too skittish. I might have eared her down the other day. Damn, thinking about that palaver with her sure got me on the prod. Change of plan. I'll step in Johnson's Fine Liquors and get me some red-eye, and then sashay on over to Maiden Lane for a spell.

A bell tinkled as Jack opened the door of the shop. "Hey, Johnson, need some snake medicine."

"Jack, you bowlegged so and so, where ya' been?" Johnson pulled a fifth of his finest whiskey and dusted it off.

Jack shook his head. "Nah. You know me better than that. Gimme some of your rotgut there. Pint'll do. Just enough to prime the pump."

"Oh, sauce for a quail."

"You got it, pal."

Jack paid him and sauntered north. I'm glad I exchanged the temptations of the Congress Hall Saloon for those at Maiden Lane. Save a bundle too, if I leave them poker games alone. Be a good chunk of money coming in when I've finished this job for Ned. Maybe enough to get me started on my dream. I aim to get a piece of land somewheres and settle down before I'm too old a pisser to enjoy what's at the end of the trail.

Two blocks east of Meyer Street, Teresa trudged up Stone Avenue, shifting from hand to hand the carpet bag of books she was returning to the library. Shops were beginning to close for afternoon siesta. Each Friday at noon, she walked to Tucson's City Hall that housed a public library on its second floor.

The afternoon sun was scorching, and beneath her arms sweat stained her plumb-colored dress. The pleasure of choosing new books at the library had no power to dispel her dismal mood. Jack hadn't called at the Emporium for almost two weeks. She had given far too much substance to her dreams, she thought. It would have been better if they had remained nebulous castles in the sky, seen from a distance. But now the misery of unrealized hope loomed larger than life across her horizon. Why, in God's name, hadn't Jack visited her?

At Congress Street, she remembered her other errand: picking up a photograph for Luis, a gift for his wife's birthday. Now he couldn't complain if she was a trifle late in returning. She waited for the horse-drawn trolley to pass before she crossed the tracks and climbed the stairs of a red brick building to Henry Buehman's Elite Studio on the second floor. She was relieved that he hadn't closed his doors for afternoon siesta.

"Good day, Miss Velarde." Henry's German accent rendered his words as "goot tay."

"Good day to you, sir. Do you have any more of those baby pictures, the Tucson babies you put together?" She leaned her heavy carpetbag against the counter's base and mopped her face with a handkerchief before placing both hands on the cool glass countertop.

"Ja, most certainly." From under the counter the photographer brought out a box with a large glossy photograph attached to the top, the composite photograph of Tucson's babies he had created. "I'm so proud of all our new citizens. Our future leaders these children will be, and even the president of the United States maybe is here."

"My goodness, you have photographed hundreds of babies!"

"Ja, better than four hundred," Henry said proudly. "A work of love it was."

"My niece and nephew are in here, Luisa and Alejandro. But I don't expect you can remember all the children's names."

"No, not all, but those two I remember. Luis's kindern. Here, I show you." He pointed to a pair of chubby faces near the lower right corner. "Such sweet faces, like anchels. Schön."

"They are not always angels, I assure you. It's a lovely photograph, Mr. Buehman."

He opened the box. "How many do you want?"

"Just one, thank you." Teresa dug in her carpetbag for the coins Luis had given her.

At the courthouse Teresa climbed the steps and stopped for breath. This trek was usually a dreaded ordeal until she reached the library on the second floor and fell under its spell, the magic of shelves filled with books. So many! And the cool and musty smell of the room—a pleasant change from the dust and dung of the streets—enchanted her. As a child, a stick of sugarcane that her Papá purchased from Sonoran carreteros had delighted her no more. The sweet taste of books! How to choose a few from the many? How to keep the load light enough to carry? She must find a good book or two to transport her, to reap moments of forgetfulness. Of peace. Of return to humdrum existence. Perhaps without Jack. At that thought a taste of bile rose to her throat, and she quickly chose her books and walked back to the Emporium.

After work Teresa returned to the casita, behind the casa grande where Luis and his family lived. Built for Luis and Olivia years earlier, the cottage included a kitchen, bedroom, and parlor, where Jessie's curtained bed and wardrobe occupied a corner opposite the beehive fireplace. In another corner Teresa's ebonized piano with a hand-carved floral pattern provided family harmony; Luis and his children crowded around it on some evenings, Manuela and Stella playing the violin, and Little Hector the guitar like his father. Luis generously allowed Teresa to leave work early on Thursdays to give piano lessons to chubby little Federico.

Following the birth of his third child, Luis had moved Teresa and Jessie to the casita during one of his stepmother's sick spells. His possession of the casa grande, the home that was Jessie's by right, embittered her. Referring to his high-handedness as "Luis's Grand Theft," Jessie didn't speak to him for weeks after the forced move. Now that Luis and Olivia had six children, the casa grande's rooms buzzed with life like a swarm of bees in the yellow-blossomed palo verde tree in the patio. Jessie's love for her grandchildren softened her attitude over the years. She and Luis called a truce, although they sometimes exchanged barbs.

Teresa found her mother reclining on her favorite chair by the parlor window with their pregnant calico cat, Chloe, on her lap. Good, Teresa thought, if Jessie was out of bed she had neared the end of her illness. The long sleeves of her ruffled white cotton wrapper hid her scarred right arm, and she sat with her left side turned to the door to hide the drawn red flesh on the right side of her face. Teresa knew nothing of the history of these scars, learning as a child never to ask. That question was certain to propel her mother into a frenzy that inevitably ended up as days spent in bed with a debilitating headache.

"I'm so glad you are feeling better today, Jessie. Your nerve tonic must have helped." As a child Teresa had mimicked Luis who addressed his stepmother by her first name. Jessie had never discouraged the practice.

"Oh Tess, it's good you went to the library. I've nothing new to read. I do so enjoy new books."

Teresa glanced at the bowed glass doors of the bookcase filled with works of Dickens, Shakespeare, Shelley, Byron, Carlyle, and a few Waverly novels. Both women had read each book more than once. When new books came into the library, they greedily pounced on them. Teresa thought, reading has brought us hours of pleasure. I'm grateful to Jessie for instilling in me a passion for reading. The most positive exchanges between us are discussions of books we read.

As she piled books on the small table by her mother's chair, Chloe jumped down heavily with a meow, stretched, and arched her back.

"Tess, did you bring me the new issue of the *National Magazine?*" Jessie asked.

"Oh no, I forgot. I did bring you a volume of Robert Browning's poetry and a book by Dickens we don't own that I thought you'd enjoy."

Jessie frowned. "How could you forget my magazine? I ask so little of you."

Teresa selected the book she wanted to read and headed for her bedroom, Chloe following her. "No, Jessie, you ask a great deal," Teresa muttered under her breath. "I take care of you on the days when you lounge about as an invalid."

She didn't plan to read then, knowing she must get up soon

to heat beans and slice ham, bread, and tomatoes for supper. She stretched out on her bed to close her eyes for a few moments, and Chloe climbed up to curl up with her head on Teresa's chest. Sleep eluded her on most of these hot June nights as she fretted over Jack, and by late afternoon she dragged along like the burro pulling Señora Aurelia's tamale cart.

Almost asleep, Teresa heard Jessie move to the kitchen table.

"Tess, just listen to this. Dickens is such a master of wit and style." In a high-pitched voice Jessie read from *The Pickwick Papers*. A few words about bugles, coaches, and Mr. Weller reached Teresa before she drifted off to sleep. She awoke with a start when Jessie shook her arm and asked if they shouldn't do something about supper.

They ate their evening meal at a drop-leaf table by Jessie's chair in the parlor, Chloe sitting expectantly at their feet. Teresa rewarded her; her mother disapproved. The windows and the door were open to catch a breeze, if there was one. Gleeful squeals of the children drifted through the open door as they played chase and tag in the patio. Going to the doorway, Jessie called out, "Children, why don't you play a quiet game for a bit?"

"They're only children, Jessie." Teresa knew that neighborhood children whispered about Jessie, calling her hechicera, an epithet that had never reached Jessie's ears. Her grandchildren defended her; to them she was a beloved grandmother, not a witch who cast evil spells. Despite her semi-invalidism, they often enjoyed happy moments with her. If they were quiet, they might sit on her lap, and she gave them hard candies to suck. For her granddaughters she dressed dolls with clothes she made from scraps of dress material. For the boys she had sewn and stuffed toy animals. When her grandchildren asked about her scarred face, she was surprisingly forbearing, explaining that it was her special mark, like a brand on a calf.

Through the open doorway Teresa glimpsed Manuela in her long apron officiously lining up the younger children at the washbasin on the back porch. No doubt, she and Olivia had supper on the table. Only fifteen, Manuela was already her mother's mainstay. The noise from the patio subsided for a time, but after supper the uproar started again, the children making the most of the long twilit evenings.

They shrieked hilariously as they played a rough and tumble game of el chicote, snap-the-whip.

Teresa lit a coal oil lamp after supper. Though daylight still lingered outside, little found its way inside the casita. Her sewing basket beside her, Jessie settled into her overstuffed chair to piece a quilt. With Chloe on her lap, Teresa sat in a matching chair and began her library book, George Eliot's *Mill on the Floss*. The description of the verdant countryside around the mill enchanted her, a cool vision on a hot June evening. But after a few pages Teresa closed her eyes, set the book down, and absentmindedly stroked Chloe as she thought of Jack.

"Olivia teaches them few manners," Jessie complained, interrupting her daughter's reverie. "At this hour Olivia should tell the children a story to prepare them for bed. She should take the youngest to the plaza to play during the morning. Of an afternoon they should nap. You and Margaret always did."

Teresa opened her book again, a hint to her mother. But Jessie, in one of her rare talking moods, chattered on. "Socorro always used to agree with me about afternoon naps."

"I remember," Teresa said. . . Ah, the afternoon siesta, the sacred rite on torrid summer afternoons. Tía Socorro sprinkling water from the olla on the tattered comforters spread on the bedroom floor to cool their hot bodies. Floors of hard-packed earth covered with canvas, except in the parlor where Jessie's Axminster carpet was spread over newspapers—the children weren't allowed to sleep on her precious carpet. Then the railroad had come to Tucson, lowering the price of lumber. The flurry and excitement of putting in wooden floors. Oh, the many luxuries those strings of boxcars had brought to town. . . .

"And now they should be in bed," Jessie was saying.

The lamp was smoking, and Teresa turned down the wick. They heard Olivia calling the children in to get ready for bed, and the patio grew quiet except for crickets chirping.

"At last they're going in, but it will take them a while to settle down to sleep. They'll whisper and laugh on the porch for another hour, the screaming little Apaches."

Teresa didn't respond; no need to encourage a tirade about Indians or Mexicans, races that were equally without merit in her mother's view. How did Jessie ever come to marry Papá? she wondered. Perhaps because he was so handsome. She glanced at the photograph of the Velarde family in its curlicued iron frame on the serape-draped piano.

Teresa recalled the day the photograph was taken. With glistening black hair and neatly trimmed mustache, her father's lips curled in an engaging smile, the all-night drinking bouts yet to mar his face. Ramrod-straight, his hand on her shoulder, he stood behind Jessie who sat in a carved wooden chair with her left side facing the camera. Dark and thin, Luis stood next to his father. Beside her mother, Teresa wore her first communion dress that was by then far too small for her. As sober and stiff as a wary cottontail rabbit, Margarita was next to her wearing a rose-colored silk gown that Teresa remembered; she had it cut down for her sister, tacking on the new white lace collar and sleeve bands she'd crocheted.

September 17, 1867 ~ A man came by in a cart & took our picture today. Papá told Luis bring out a chair for Mamá. Luis said, ella no es mi madre. Good thing Papá didn't hear him say Jessie wasn't his mother or he would have skinned him. Papá's first wife died when Luis was born. For the picture we all stood by the grape vine ramada. The grape leaves made shadows on the ground and I was finding animal faces in them. Papá told me to hold my head up. The clothes on the line blew off and I put them back in the wash tub. Margarita was afraid of the picture man under the black cover and she was crying. In the picture Papá is the only one smiling.

Teresa's gaze shifted to her mother, who leaned into the circle of light cast by the coal oil lamp as she pieced a scrap of rose-colored silk into her crazy quilt. "Jessie, that scrap was from your dress. Margarita is wearing that dress in this photograph. Do you remember it?" She pointed to the portrait.

Jessie let her sewing fall to her lap. "Of course I remember it. I always hated it."

"Why, Jessie?" As their eyes met, a shiver slid down Teresa's spine.

Her mother failed to answer. Teresa, used to her moody silences, didn't press her. But she noticed her mother's lips moving as they sometimes did when she was rehashing the past.

In her bedroom Teresa changed into a cambric nightgown and thrust a small wooden wedge under her bedroom door, a precaution she took each night to ensure privacy. She moved the chamber pot beneath her bed—she knew her mother would never touch it. Behind it was a carton with her diaries. She removed two, one old and her newest made of tan duck cloth with corners and spine of Russian leather. Seated at her bedside table, she licked the end of her pencil, and wrote.

June 19, 1891 ~ When Jack first came into the store he asked my given name. I have so many. Jessie calls me Tess. Papá used to call me Palomita and Tía Socorro does. I must be some sort of fowl for Luis sometimes calls me chihui, turkey. As a child I took the part of a turkey in a school play. Luis laughed & took great pleasure in yelling 'gobble gobble' at me. He said I was big and awkward. He still calls me Chihui when he is angry at me.

It has been 12 days since I saw Mr. Jack O'Brien. Oh God, I do pray that our friendship continues.

Chloe scratched at the door and Teresa let her in, replacing the wedge. She propped her pillow against the brass headboard and climbed into bed. With the cat by her side she flipped through the pages of the older diary and randomly chose an entry. She had recently started to read through them. Anything to take her mind from Jack.

October 12, 1879 ~ Went to a band concert at Fort Lowell with Mercedes. We sat on chairs on the parade ground & after the concert two soldiers talked to us. Corp. Charles Samuels, asked me to walk down the lane with him. He asked if he could come to see me. I said yes. Then the wagon we came in had to rush back before dark because Apaches might attack.

Oct. 18, 1879 ~ I found Jessie reading my diary. I'm furious. She said it was a mother's right to gather information about her daughter. She scolded me for seeing a man in secret. I yelled at her, I'm 25 years old. Why won't you allow me to have a suitor? She told me not to moon over the likes of him. Called him unsuitable! But she did give me permission to go to the Sunday concert at Carrillo's Gardens with Miss Grafton.

Miss Penelope Grafton was one of the few Tucsonans Jessie Velarde respected. Teresa thought her piano teacher wore a corset of steel and strong spectacles that missed no errant fingering. Miss Grafton maintained that Carrillo's concerts were the only oases in Tucson's musical desert and insisted they were part of her students' training. That day she merely sniffed at Teresa's timid suggestion that they might attend the band concert at Fort Lowell instead. "No, we go to Carrillo's Gardens. The cacophony produced by a band may be suitable for marching soldiers, but it is not music."

Not even the performance of a Bach prelude and fugue—a work in Teresa's repertoire—penetrated her cloud of gloom. During the concert her mind drifted back to the Fort Lowell band concert. She wistfully remembered how Corporal Samuels had held her hand as they parted. And now someone had wanted to hold her hand again. But what had happened to him?

Teresa readjusted her pillow and scooted up in bed to read one more entry.

Dec. 1 1879 ~ "True hospitality neither expects nor desires any return, and it is only the inhospitable that keep a debt and credit account." I found this in the "Ladies' Companion" the other day. Miss Grafton says this in her own way. Once when I thanked her for giving me extra time at my lesson she said, "Now, Teresa, you need not thank me. It is my pleasure or I would not do so. I am not a timekeeper, nor a bookkeeper." She is so kind to me.

How strange life has turned out, Teresa thought. Now I am both a bookkeeper and a timekeeper, and my piano is sadly neglected. Moths batted against the lamp, startling her from her reverie. She disturbed the cat as she slipped out of bed to hide the diaries under it and slide the wedge from under the door. She cupped her hand over the lamp and blew out the flame, the golden afterglow shimmering against her eyelids as she settled back in bed. I won't dream of Corporal Samuels tonight as I used to all those years ago, but will I dream of Jack? Am I one of those moths futilely beating against a barrier of glass?

5 San Agustín ❖ June 21, 1891

At dawn on Sunday the heat was suffocating, and Teresa didn't take her usual horseback ride. Instead, she walked with Luis and his family to San Agustín for mass, the women decked out in hats and gloves. As they walked up Convent Street—less likely to be filled with carts and buggies than Stone—Manuela and Stella, on either side of three-year-old Luisa, clasped her hands, periodically lifting her for a few steps. Each swoop elicited squeals of delight.

The three Velarde boys, Hector, Federico, and Alejandro, raced ahead, ignoring their parents' repeated instructions to walk, not run. Chubby Alejandro couldn't keep up with his older brothers and soon fell back to walk beside his mother. Olivia took his hand, her other plump arm looped through her husband's. Luis smiled and waved at passersby. Teresa knew this Sunday morning routine was designed to maintain the polish on his image.

When the family reached La Plaza de Mesilla, Teresa lingered to gaze at the two church towers, one domed and one pointed, both surmounted by a cross. The rose window above the entrance, added a few years ago, marked the edifice as a cathedral. She had sketched the scene as a child. She should do it again, she thought. Once in the church, she automatically observed the formalities of the mass, unable to banish images of the picnic and the misery of Jack's apparent disinterest in her.

At home, Jessie, who always claimed she would never darken the door of a Catholic church, was up and about. She invaded Olivia's kitchen—once her own realm, she often grumbled—to complete the meal that Olivia and Manuela had begun earlier. After church the family trooped in, the children clamoring for dinner. Luis said grace and everyone tucked into roast chicken, frijoles, their own garden squash, onions, and tomatoes, accompanied by a basket of warm tortillas. The day before, Manuela had made empanadas de calabasa, pumpkin turnovers, for dessert. After eating the fritters with cinnamon and brown sugar syrup, most of the family headed off to their siestas.

Teresa helped Manuela and Stella wash dishes before she fetched her sketchpad from the casita and sat on the splintery bench in the ramada. Splotches of sun leaked through the leaves above and fell on her page as she sketched the palo verde tree with its fallen blossoms yellowing the dusty earth beneath it. The stuccoed and whitewashed adobe walls radiated heat, turning the garden into an oven, even in the shade of the grapevine. Exasperated and enervated, she went into the casita to stretch out on her bed. She picked up *The Mill on the Floss*. She was only a few pages into it.

The words blurred and her eyes glazed over. As she let the book flop down on her chest, she heard a train whistle, as it rattled and clattered on the nearby track that cut diagonally across the east side of town. The Southern Pacific had run to Tucson for a decade, transforming it from a frontier village of mud and dust, its streets rife with drunkenness and daily shootings, to a growing and more prosperous town. Concerned citizens were presently enacting laws to ensure safety and orderly growth.

Ironically, the iron wheels that click-clacked over the shining rails had ruined some pioneer Tucson merchants as surely as they had become the wheels of progress for others. With the influx of cheaper goods from the railroads, freighters like Pinckney Tully and Estevan Ochoa went bankrupt. The Emporium, then located on Meyer Street, nearly went under during that period, but Luis had shrewdly kept his prices ruinously low until he unloaded his shelves. Fortunately, Luis Velarde had no fine house or lifestyle to maintain like some of Tucson's merchant princes. Yet, it was a few years before he again turned a profit.

Industriousness could have been Luis's middle name. He often bragged to Teresa that he was only fourteen when he left school to work at Solomon Warner's store. Next, he sold his own merchandise from a makeshift stall on West Congress Street, always bringing his earnings home to Jessie, who saw to it that Hector received no money to waste on drink.

Hector had died when Luis was nineteen. Luis urged his stepmother to invest her widow's pension in his growing business in exchange for putting food on her table. Jessie obliged him, knowing she had little choice. Luis rented a small adobe building on Meyer Street, and forced Teresa to keep books for him. His shrewd business sense soon resulted in improvements to their lives. Instead of the occasional chicken, Luis's new bride, Olivia, could put a cut of beef on the table on feast days.

Four years ago, a windfall had enabled Luis to buy a larger building on Stone Avenue. In Mexico his grandmother, Doña Verlarde, bestowed generous legacies upon her heirs. Luis persuaded Teresa to invest hers in the new store. On paper she had part interest in the venture, but other than a pitifully small monthly salary, she had received no return of capital. Though Teresa complained, Luis merely made vague promises of future dividends or trotted out the usual litany of his saving the family from destitution by his hard work. He grumbled that St. Joseph's School had never returned the remainder of her tuition when he had pulled her out before the term was over. She must make restitution for that loss, he told her.

Luis never intended to return her investment, Teresa thought, and from what he paid her she had managed to save only eighty dollars. She would like to turn her hand at something besides bookkeeping, perhaps teaching school; she needed to complete her education, perhaps at the new university northwest of town, but that took money. Luis would howl if she tried to leave the Emporium. There was no way she could escape this trap—until now. Squaring her shoulders, she vowed to fight for Jack.

6 Tía Socorro ❖ June 22

Monday morning, another weary workday, Teresa complained to herself in her sweltering office at the Emporium. At noon she heard voices in the back patio. Assuming that Luis and his hired man, Lito, had returned from the depot with a shipment of new merchandise, she locked the front door for the usual siesta closure and went out to help. To her surprise she found Lito handing Tía Socorro Velarde down from the wagon laden with the new shipment. Her butterball figure, akin to his, challenged him as she stepped onto the wooden box he had placed beside the wagon. He steadied her with a wrinkled brown hand, still strong despite his girth and age.

With a loud "whoosh" Socorro landed on the box, nearly splintering it. "¡Hola, Palomita!"

"¡Tía Socorro! How good to see you. I didn't know you were coming. You usually come in August for the Fiesta."

"Te queria sorprender, dear niece," Socorro said with a chuckle.

"You *did* surprise me. Bienvenida, Tía Socorro. Welcome!"

The two women embraced, Socorro kissing and patting Teresa's cheeks. For decades her father's maiden sister had lived in Sonora but appeared like an angel of mercy before the birth of each of her brother's children. A life-giving force in Teresa's eyes, she was like the Santa Cruz River.

"You didn't come last year." Teresa's tone was accusing. "I wish you'd move to Tucson."

"My home is in Tubutama, Palomita. Last summer I had to stay home to repair my roof, but we shall have a good long visit this time."

Teresa turned to Lito. "¿Donde está Luis?"

"Fué al banco," the old Yaqui Indian replied with a sly smile.

"Oh, he stopped at the bank, did he?" Teresa winked at him. "I do the banking. You mean Luis has stopped off at the Congress Hall Saloon to play a game or two of faro with his friends." And polish his business contacts, she added to herself.

As they walked into the store, Teresa hugged her aunt again. "I'm so glad you are here. We must have a good chat later. But now I need to check the bills of lading with Lito and then run to the bank—the real bank. Do you mind watching the shop for a while?"

"Claro que no. Of course not, querida. It makes me feel like I'm back in harness, just like old times. Go along and take care of your business."

Socorro was straightening a shelf of ladies' boots when she heard the doorbell tinkle.

"Buenas tardes, Señora. ¿Señora—?" A burly man in the doorway removed his hat and stroked his bushy blond mustache.

"Velarde, señor. Buenas tardes." Socorro didn't correct him about her matrimonial state.

"Mucho gusto. I'm Jack O'Brien. I have the honor to be acquainted with your daughter, Señorita Velarde. She is a fine woman."

Amused by Señor O'Brien's assumption she was Teresa's mother, Socorro said nothing to amend his second mistake. Solamente dios sabe, only God in Heaven knows, she thought, she'd been more a mother to her brother's children than Jessie had.

Jack poked his head into Teresa's office. "I see she's not here. Would you please tell her I stopped in?"

"But of course, Señor O'Brien, con mucho gusto."

She decided he carried himself well for a large man. ¿Y qué tenemos aquí? What have we here? ¿Un romance? Socorro decided she must ask her niece.

After work Teresa and Socorro started for home, Teresa carrying her aunt's valise. They paused as a Mexican woodcutter with a cartload of mesquite firewood slowly ground down Stone Avenue, stirring up dust. The cart was followed by a pair of bicycle riders.

Socorro turned to Teresa with a broad smile. "¿Quién es este Señor O'Brien?"

"Señor O'Brien? You saw him? He came in today?"

"Sí, mi amor. He came to the Emporium while you were at the bank."

She had missed him! For an instant Teresa felt as though she'd been stabbed with a knife, but the next moment she was elated. Jack *had* come to see her. "Today makes four times he has visited the store," she said. Then she bit her lip. Ay dios mío, why make it so obvious she was keeping count? She attempted to quell her trembling, glancing at her aunt to see if she had noticed her reaction.

As their eyes met, Socorro smiled. "Could this be an affair of the heart? Dime, Palomita, tell me something about your galán. Who is he?"

"Oh, he's just someone I met. Works down at Rancho Dos Colinas. I barely know him. . . Tía Socorro, let's go to Manny's. You love ice cream. We'll celebrate your visit." Teresa hoped to end the inquisition, but suspected her canny old aunt read her face.

At Manny's Ice Cream Parlor on Cushing Street they each ordered a dish of ice cream, and as Teresa lifted a spoonful to her lips, she recalled her first taste of the luscious confection.

June 28, 1869 ~ My 15th birthday. Papá wanted me to have a debut, a Quinceñera at church but Jessie wouldn't allow it, so for a celebration he brought home some Ice Cream. Jessie was mad and he went slinking off, to a saloon, I guess. This was my first taste of Ice Cream. It's wonderful but I didn't know I must put it back in the icebox. It turned all runny and Jessie flew into a screaming rage. She hit my head and back with a broom. I bent over & tried to shield my face, then I got boiling mad & hit her back. I am taller. We were both crying & I said I was sorry. She went to bed but later she told me she was sorry too. Guess I have sinned, but I don't care. I don't think she will try to beat me again.

Teresa slid a spoon of strawberry ice cream into her mouth. "It's so delicious. . . Tía Socorro. I don't think you ever laid a hand on me. Did you?"

"No, nunca, not on any of you. That was not my way. ¿Porqué preguntas?"

"Oh, just thinking back. Your scoldings were certainly different from Jessie's. Remember when I found a horny toad? When we lived by the Presidio? I put it in a little box and showed it to you."

"No, I can't remember it. A pasado mucho tiempo."

"You scolded me for keeping it and marched me across the road, made me let it go. For the rest of the afternoon I sat under the mesquite tree by the street, chewing and spitting out bean pods, pouting, I guess." Now and then, Teresa mused, I still pull a pod from the mesquite tree in our patio and suck on it. Like ice cream, which tastes of triumph, the sweet juice of the bean reminds me of Socorro's rare rebuke, a memory far more vivid than Jessie's abuse.

As they walked home, Teresa asked, "Tía Socorro, I know Papá served in the Mexican garrison at Tubaca and was mustered out of the army before I was born. But how did he end up living in Tucson?"

"While my brother was still in Tubaca, he married a young girl, Manuela. She died giving birth to Luis, and soon afterward Hector married Jessie. After you were born your papá came here to start a new life. He found a job as a blacksmith at Sweeney's. Then he sent for me to help Jessie cope with two babies. After all, she was only eighteen."

"And Luis was not even her own baby. So I was born in Tubaca?" Teresa asked.

"Sí. Tu eres mi niña de La Venta de la Mesilla."

"The Gadsden Purchase."

"You were born in 1854, the year that treaty was approved." Socorro shook her head. "My family was stolen away along with el norte de Sonora by un tal americano, Gadsden, and a few marks on a paper."

"I have no memory of Tubaca, but I remember our first house in Tucson. Doors of saguaro ribs tied together with twigs, and windows covered only with strips of rawhide."

"To keep flies out. With those stables across the way we had an awful time with las moscas. ¡Madre de Dios! We had flies! Impossible to keep them off you and your sister."

Teresa had been told her father built the two-room house using adobes from the old Presidio walls. He eventually added another room and installed glass windows. A few years later he traded the town lot—not the house itself—for property on Sixth Avenue, an area of creosote bushes, sand, and desert. Along with their father, Luis and Teresa removed the glass windows, frames and doors from the house and then tore down the walls to salvage the adobes. Loading the material on a cart and unloading it at the new site took many trips. It was backbreaking work.

"I remember you came to help us move," Teresa said. "We lived in a tent for a while."

"You were a good-sized girl then, and your father said you worked just as hard as Luis." Socorro turned to smile at her niece. "You tramped around in mud and straw in your bare feet to help Lito make more adobes. ¿Te acuerdas?"

"Sí, I remember, it was fun." Teresa smiled as she recalled the delight of squishing wet earth and straw between her toes. But she sobered at the memory of the events that followed the new house's completion. Jessie had demanded privacy because of her headaches and insisted that her husband add an adobe wall to divide their bedroom in two. After that, his hard drinking began, and in the next months he lost his blacksmithing job at Sweeney's.

Socorro said, "It was a hot summer when the house was finished. You and Margarita were so afraid of Apaches you wouldn't sleep outside. But you girls were safe enough with the army right beside you at Fort Lowell."

"It was called Camp Lowell then. Everyone complained about those rowdy soldiers smack in the middle of Tucson. Finally the army moved out to the desert northeast of town."

"Ah yes, I remember now."

"The new house seemed so large. That's why Papá named it the casa grande. After Luis and Olivia married and Manuela was born, the house became crowded again, and Lito helped us build the casita. But I never knew how Luis found the money for that."

"It wasn't his, Palomita. Do you think he would dole out money he could use for his business? Olivia used her dowry for the casita."

The two women pushed through the sagging gate in the ocotillo fence behind the Velarde patio. Teresa was certain that no matter how dark the night, their privy's smell could have guided them home.

At the casita they found Jessie in bed, the curtain closed. Teresa pulled it back and said softly, "Jessie, look who's here."

"Socorro," Jessie whispered. "I'm pleased to see you."

Socorro bent to kiss Jessie's forehead. Teresa was always surprised at her mother's attachment to Tía Socorro. Though Jessie alienated most people of Mexican descent—often her stepson—Tía Socorro was an exception. Like the leavening she used in her bread dough, her sister-in-law always seemed to lighten Jessie's life.

June 25, 1878 ~ Not much sleep for me last night. Wanted to sleep outside in the patio, but it rained. Went back to the porch with Luis and Olivia, babies and all. Little María is sick & cried all night. Tía Socorro and Olivia nursed her. Dia de San Juan Fiesta is here and the streets are full of shouting & gunfire & drunks riding up and down. It was impossible to sleep. The night of San Juan's Day is not a good time in Tucson. This morning I found out Pablo Ramirez was killed in a fight last night. His poor Family, what will they do?

July 2, 1878 ~ Little María died last night. Dr. Handy came but could not help her. It was the Small Pox. Half the children in Tucson have it. Olivia is taking it very hard & cannot stop crying. We worried about Manuela. Doctor Handy told us she doesn't have any signs of it & he gave her a vaccination. Luis asked me to pick out a little coffin at Perez's. Poor little one, only a year old last month, dear sweet baby. Tía Socorro has been a saint, helping Jessie with the housework and cooking our meals.

Except for Jessie who kept to her bed, that evening the family gathered in the ramada to sing with Luis accompanying the songs on his guitar. After the family retired, Teresa lingered there, staring up at the grape leaves silhouetted against the fading blue twilight in the west. A few doves still strutted and cooed under the palo verde before they joined the others perching in the tree for their rest. Teresa softly sang a verse of a song the family had sung earlier that evening: "Ven, Ven, amor / que triste estoy; / sin ti no hay luz / ni alumbra el sol."*

---

* "Come, come, my love, / I am so blue; / without you there is no light / and the sun does not shine."

As the stars appeared, the children stretched out on their mattresses on the porch; tired out, their chatter soon faded. In the iron grip of suffocating heat, Teresa could scarcely breathe or summon the energy to go to bed. It will be another long, hot night, she thought. Ah, she then recalled, Jack had tried to visit her that day. That cooled her like a breeze.

7 The Letter ❖ June 23

. . . Restless dreams pulled at her. Black-veiled women gently sobbed in the dark. A carriage draped in black drifted by on silent wheels. Hushed, contemplative murmurs insistently repeated, mingled with low moaning. She lay in a sealed sepulcher. . . .

In thrall to the terrifying nightmare, Teresa struggled to open her eyes, but they seemed glued shut. With a final desperate effort she rolled away from the wall and opened them. Bright sunlight poured through her window, casting a shadow of her pitcher and basin on the rag rug by her bed.

"Mercy! Thank goodness my terrible nightmare awoke me," she cried out, sitting up. "It's past sunup. I'm late to work." She sprang up to wash at her basin and hurry into her clothes. Brisk action helped to tear away the nightmare's tattered shrouds. Such dreams haunted her most nights, and by day she couldn't seem to order her thoughts. She yearned to confide in Tía Socorro, but couldn't imagine telling her of picnicking with Jack without a chaperon. Dear as she was, her aunt was even more conventional than her mother.

She pulled on her shoes, listening to the mourning dove's plaintive *coo-coo, coo-coo-coo,* realizing it was the sound she mistook for her own sobbing in her dream. To her, the soothing call was not mournful. After all, it was the song of the courting male. She drew a long breath, her nighttime phantoms almost dispelled, and gazed out her window to search the palo verde tree for the feathered suitor. She saw no sign of him, but the activity in the sunny patio cheered her. Washday for the Velarde family. Olivia was stoking a fire under the five-gallon coal oil can used for boiling water. Socorro, at the well with a galvanized tin pail that reflected dazzling light into Teresa's sleepy eyes, was drawing water to fill two zinc laundry tubs for rinsing. On the porch of the casa grande Manuela sorted clothes into piles. Two washboards leaning against the washhouse glinted in the sun. Teresa shook her head; Manuela would cry over her red hands after this day's work.

The Emporium door swung open before Teresa could unlock it. Luis's dark eyes narrowed and his facial muscles tightened in fury, he growled, "You were to be here an hour ago to help me with the inventory. Are you ill?"

"No, I overslept."

"Overslept? Well, you certainly take your duties lightly." Luis locked the door behind her.

Teresa shrugged and started for her office. He stepped in front of her, his hands clenched. "Chihui, you were seen riding with that lowlife, O'Brien. My own sister consorting with a cowhand. In the name of God, what were you thinking of? Sneaking around behind my back. What have you become?"

Ay dios mío, he knows about the picnic, Teresa thought. That busybody customer who had seen them on the road to San Xavier must have told him. Shrinking under Luis's hawklike gaze, her breath caught in her throat, she stared at him.

"By being seen with that scum you sullied the Velarde name, the name I've worked so hard to make respectable."

"Jack—Mr. O'Brien is not scum! And what I do is my own business." Teresa shouted back. "I am thirty-seven-years old. And you are not my keeper."

She pushed past him, but he grabbed her arm and spun her around. "I *am* your keeper. And I try to maintain our good name. You are not ever to see this man again."

"Take your hands off me! I'll see him if I please." Her arms rigid at her sides, she breathed out slowly, thinking, he doesn't know of the picnic or he'd have already spit it out.

"What do you want people to think, Chihui? That you are a puta de la calle, a street whore?"

Teresa slapped her stepbrother's face.

His hand on his cheek, he hissed at her, "You shouldn't have done that. I shall ride out to Dos Colinas and shoot the bastard!"

"Luis, please don't talk so wildly." Desperation gripped her at the thought of a confrontation between Jack and her stepbrother. "Pardon me. I lost my temper. Please, let's talk."

"Nothing to talk about. That lowlife is a womanizer, a liar, a cheat, a braggart—"

"How can you say that? You don't know him at all."

"I have run into him enough times. On Congress Street. And, believe me, I know his type well."

Had her stepbrother been bested by Jack at cards? she wondered. She said in a calmer voice, "Very well, Luis, I'll be guided by your wishes. Just do not ride down there when you are so angry. Something terrible might happen; you'd regret it the rest of your days. I'll write a letter to Mr. O'Brien, ask him to come to town and talk with you."

"Talking won't bring back your reputation, or our good name. Do you know how hard it has been for me to clear the Velarde name after Papá became the town drunk?"

"Papá was not the town drunk! He had been a brave soldier. Everyone knows—" Teresa instantly moderated her tone. "Luis, will you be content if I write to Jack? I promise not to see him until you talk with him. I'll write him this very evening."

Whatever Luis might have answered was lost when two well-dressed women appeared at the Emporium's window and peered in. He glanced at the clock and hastened to unlock the door. The sight of prospective customers doused the flames more effectively than any words of reason Teresa might have summoned. She escaped to her office to compose herself.

Luis pointedly avoided her the rest of the day. As he locked up that evening, he said, "Send your letter down to O'Brien with Lito in the morning, though that will change nothing."

She felt like snapping back, but silently followed him out of the Emporium, thinking that Luis in the role of protective brother was as strange as a rattlesnake defending a roadrunner.

Late that night after her mother was asleep, Teresa sat at her bedside table with notepaper and pen.

Dear Mr. O'Brien,

    I hope this letter finds you well. Have you had any rain on the ranch? We have had none. It has been terribly hot here. Tucson may dry up and blow away.

    I would be grateful if you would meet with me at the public library in the next few days to discuss a matter of some importance to me. Please come as soon as you find it convenient. Remember to meet me at the library, not the Emporium. Please write me today and name a date and a time to meet.

I remain your faithful friend,
Teresa

She reread the letter, finding it strained and evasive. Frowning, she nearly crumpled it up, but she couldn't spell out the reason she must see him. The letter might be seen by others. And if she had written that her stepbrother was furious about their being seen together, she might very well frighten Jack away entirely. She must meet Jack before Luis did and warn him not to speak of the picnic. Lying to Luis about not seeing Jack before they talked upset her less than the fear that Luis *would* see Jack before she did. This fear was ever present, like a cactus thorn lodged in her sleeve pricking her with every move she made.

She sighed. This would have to do. Surely, it should bring Jack to town to see what was on her mind, and, dear God, let him not come to the Emporium when he came. That was the best she could hope for. Her stomach still knotted, she placed the letter in her carpetbag. She'd hand it to Lito in the morning. Fluffing out her pillows, she settled in bed with her journal to reread the previous entries about Jack, hoping to wring a little joy from them. Ah, he had paid another visit to the Emporium yesterday. That was joy in itself.

Chloe scratched at her bedroom door. Teresa opened it, and the cat waddled in, barely able to spring up to the bed. Teresa hid the journal and blew out the lamp. She whispered to her cat, "I wasn't honest in my diary. Perhaps I'm not even being honest about this romance. Is it a romance, or is it just a passing fling for Jack? Chloe, is he just tomcatting around like some Romeo did with you?"

8 Jessie ❖ June 24

The next day Jessie hummed a tune as she worked in the kitchen, quite pleased with herself. She proudly centered a platter of sliced tomatoes on the wooden table and then stirred the chicken soup on the stove. When Teresa came home for supper, she greeted her with a cheerful, "Hello, Tess."

"Something certainly smells good," Teresa said. "Where did you get the tomatoes? Ours aren't ripe yet."

"Sam Wong. He came by today."

For years the Velarde family had bought vegetables from Tucson's Chinese gardeners. Dressed in loose pants and shirts, their pushcarts laden with potatoes, onions, corn, lettuce, and carrots, they sold from door to door. They kept track of purchases by scrawling their strange symbols on customers' doorframes. Most extended credit, collecting their money on an appointed day.

"I'm glad you are up and about, Jessie. I see you've been busy today."

"Yes, I baked bread this morning." Jessie pulled out a loaf from the pie safe, removing the white cloth with a flourish before she set it on the table. "Tess, come with me. You have a surprise in your bedroom."

A basket lay near Teresa's bed. Smiling a cat smile and purring loudly, Chloe lay curled around four nursing kittens, one calico and three black. "Oh Chloe, you're a mother!" Teresa stroked the cat's head and tremulously touched the bobbing head of each tiny kitten.

"They're sweet when they're small," Jessie said as they returned to the kitchen. "Tess, would you lay a place for Socorro? She'll be over directly. And get down a jar of molasses? In Kansas, we used to beg Mama for 'bread and 'lasses.' It was a great treat for us."

"You seem to be feeling well today, Jessie."

"Yes, I feel quite sprightly, thank goodness." Jessie cut thick slices of bread. "But you've been looking peaked lately, Tess. Anything wrong?"

"Oh no. It's the heat, and I'm tired because we've started that cussed inventory at the store."

"Ah, here's Socorro." Her face glistening with sweat, Jessie dished up the vegetable soup.

In the parlor after supper Jessie sat in her armchair with her scarred face turned away from the room. She pieced scraps of material together for a quilt, and Socorro embroidered a pillowcase.

Teresa sat stroking Chloe, who was taking a break from motherhood. "Today customers were abuzz with gossip. Dr. Handy's trying to have Mary evicted from their home. Don't know how he can do it legally; the court awarded it to her some time ago."

Teresa turned to her aunt. "Perhaps you haven't heard the rumors that the doctor has been beating his wife. Strange that he was the one who filed for divorce. He threatened to shoot any lawyer who defended her, but at last Frank Heney decided to take her case. It was a bitter trial that lasted eight months. Dr. Handy had already gained custody of their five children. It was terrible for him to wrench those children from Mary and send them off to California to live with his mother."

"I remember when they married. She wasn't yet seventeen," Jessie said. "I read in the paper that the Scott's garden was lit with lamps and candles and wedding guests danced long into the night." Jessie bit off a thread. "But it didn't turn out to be a happy marriage."

"I knew Mary Scott at St. Joseph's. She was a lovely girl, younger than I," Teresa said. "Everyone knows of Dr. Handy's hot temper, and it's said that he's also a wife-beater and womanizer. I can scarcely believe that. He's such a good doctor."

"Well, I hear Mary's chronically ill and, worse, she's become a morphine addict to control her pain. She had four children in four years. Two years ago there was a fifth. She was too frail and ill to bear another." Jessie turned to her sister-in-law. "Socorro, wouldn't constant childbirth rob a woman of her health?" Her needle suspended in the air, Jessie looked directly at Socorro, and muttered sotto voce, "At least I knew how to put an end to having more children."

Socorro frowned at Jessie as she placed her needlework in her satchel. "I'm sorry for the poor woman. Losing her children. Well, I must get to my bed. Buenas noches."

Awake in her curtained bed, Jessie was pleased that her supper turned out so well. The taste of molasses and bread still on her tongue sparked memories about Kansas, about the good times in her white clapboard home on Everett Street. She was the youngest of six children, born ten years after her siblings had married and moved away. She now realized that like a Kansas sunflower, she had been nurtured in the warm glow of undivided parental love and attention.

Jessie had loved to curl up with a book in some corner of the house or in a hammock in the garden among the hollyhocks. Life was filled with what she now deemed idyllic pastimes. Sledding and sleigh rides in winter; croquet on the lawn or swimming in the branch in summer. On Sundays the family, dressed in their Sunday best, walked to the white Methodist church two streets away, where her father served as a lay preacher.

She had spent many summer days at her grandparents' farm just outside of town. She fed chickens and gathered eggs, poking under clucking hens in their warm straw nests. She watched Grandpa milk cows in the barn, gleeful when he squirted milk into the mouths of a pair of cats eagerly waiting beside him. At dusk she scrambled through the long grass in the front yard of the farmhouse to catch fireflies, suffering from fiery chigger bites the next day.

At this point Jessie tried to brake her train of thoughts, but memory's momentum carried her on to the fateful day in the summer when she had turned ten. Gammie had called her out to the front yard to see a cyclone twisting ominously on the western horizon. The black funnel suddenly veered in their direction. They ran to the storm cellar under the smoke house, banging down the door and latching it. In the dark, damp cellar Jessie clung to Gammie in terror as the wind howled above them. When it grew quiet, her grandmother cautiously raised the door, just as Grandpa and the farm hands came running in from the field. Grandpa knelt on the ground to praise God they'd all escaped. Missing the house, the black funnel had torn away the roof of the barn and dropped it in the orchard before it swerved north.

Grandpa had hitched old Tomboy to the wagon, and they headed to town to find out how his son and his wife had fared in the cyclone. Much of the town lay in shambles—trees uprooted or standing as skeletons denuded of leaves, dead horses in the mud, buggies crushed against trees, collapsed houses, and furniture strewn everywhere. The devastation was heartrending. Townspeople picked through the ruins or sat on an upended piece of furniture in a daze, their head in their hands. Jessie knew them; they were friends and neighbors.

Breathless as they had approached her home, Jessie was heartened to see her house. Though it leaned drunkenly to the left, it still stood. Grandpa urged Tomboy around to the backyard. The back of the house was cleanly sliced off, and chairs, beds, and tables from the two floors had spilled into the mud. In the hole of an uprooted tree Jessie saw a flash of pink ruffle. It was her doll, her china face half buried in the mud. "Oh, Betsy," she cried as she jumped down from the wagon to pick up the doll, sobbing and hugging her to her breast, mud and all.

Jessie couldn't remember all that happened next. There had been frantic inquiries and a prolonged search for her parents. She was asleep part of the time. When they returned to the farm late that night, her grandmother led her into the parlor where Grandpa sat. "Sit down, Jessie dear," he said. "I've some hard news for you. God has taken both your parents to their heavenly rest."

Gammie had held her hand as Grandpa prayed. After his long prayer, Jessie ran upstairs to her bed. She cried and hiccuped until she made herself ill.

Now when she tried to visualize her parents, she could only see the face of her doll.

9 Vanishing Point ❖ June 27 to July 4

By Saturday Jack hadn't appeared, and Luis announced that he'd ride to Dos Colinas the next day. Teresa begged him to wait, reminding him she had sent the letter only a few days ago; it wasn't reasonable to expect Jack yet. Her plea was useless, and she was in a state of despair. When the two met, Jack would assume that Luis knew about the picnic and the fat would be in the fire.

In the long twilit evening after supper, Teresa carried two dishpans, one empty and one filled with warm soapy water, to the old wooden table on the patio under the ramada. She collected coal-oil lamps from both households. At the pump she filled the second pan with cold water.

A clean dishtowel draped over one arm, Socorro joined her. "Don't bite your lip so hard, it will bleed. ¿Qué te pasa, Palomita? You have looked quite ill these days."

"It's just that store inventory. Thank goodness, it's done now."

"Teresita, I know why you are unhappy. Luis is riding south tomorrow to confront Señor O'Brien." Socorro drew water from the well to fill the second pan. "He said you were seen with him. I tried to reason with him on your behalf, pero no me escuchaba. He called him un sinvergüenza."

"A scoundrel? Yes, he'd malign anyone who took an interest in me. Lo siento. I am sorry, Socorro. Luis and I quarreled about him. I'm so upset." Teresa threaded a soapy cloth through the lamp chimney, then scoured it with a long-handled brush. "Luis shouldn't treat me as a child. But there is no reasoning with him. I don't know what is going to happen."

Socorro rinsed the row of chimneys, drying them until they sparkled. "You can come to me with your troubles anytime, Palomita."

"Dear Tía, I know that." Teresa hugged her aunt, raising her wet hands in the air.

On Sunday morning Teresa decided to attend the Congregational Church. Tía Socorro declined an invitation to accompany her, saying she would go to San Agustín with Luis's family. Wearing her gray dress of cotton lawn and her wide-brimmed straw hat with white batiste roses on it, Teresa set off on foot. She passed by the new Plaza School, a handsome building on Fifth Avenue. Creosote bushes growing on hard-packed earth surrounded the baseball diamond in the Military Plaza. She paused before the old whitewashed adobes of the Ochoa house on Stone and Camp, and it stirred up memories.

May 4, 1870 ~ Today Sister Euphrasia took us out to sketch. She is teaching us about linear perspective. Sister said to draw one building on the street using vanishing points. I chose the Ochoa home. Made a sad botch of it. I wonder about vanishing points. If Jessie and Papá were walking on either side of a road would they meet at the vanishing point? How I long for this to happen for Jessie and Papá. Sometimes he is so sad. If I am patient perhaps they will finally come together down the road. I know if Papá were my husband I'd walk close to him.

As Teresa passed the Church Plaza, the bells of San Agustín rang out, startling a flock of pigeons on the roof. The bird cloud flapped down to the Plaza with rusty-sounding wing beats. "Silly birds, I wonder how many times a day you do that?"

The Congregational Church with its proud Gothic arches and peaked roof was originally Presbyterian, the first Protestant church in Tucson. At one time Teresa had accompanied Sunday morning hymns on its decrepit piano, but she had not been inside the church for a decade. Over the years she had sometimes attended the Catholic Church with Luis and his family, but more often she took her Sunday morning horseback rides. She guessed she was a mestizo both in her lineage and in her religion.

As she stepped through the church's tall arched doors today, she hoped it would take her mind off the scene that must be taking place at Dos Colinas between Luis and Jack. Teresa stood for the last hymn, singing, "O Jesus, thou art standing/ Outside the fast-closed door, / In lowly patience waiting/ To pass the threshold o'er . . ." Didn't she stand at a fast-closed door? She was shocked at the profane image she had conjured: she was at the door waiting for Jack. She realized that she hadn't heard a word of the lengthy sermon.

After siesta that afternoon Teresa awakened to Luis's barking laughter. *He's back!* She hurried out to the patio, her heart thumping in dread. Luis sat playing with little Luisa on the ramada's bench. How could he be so jolly, when in the twinkling of an eye he would spring on her like a lion?

"Ah, Teresa," he said with a smile. "Sit down and hear my news. Your friend has been away from the ranch for a while buying cattle in Mexico. Wes Pearson, owner of Dos Colinas, seems to hold O'Brien in high esteem."

"You sound as if you approve of Jack." Teresa's black mood evaporated. She sat beside Luis, pulling Luisa to her lap.

"Why, yes, it appears he's not a lowlife drifter after all."

"And just why did you take him for one?" That rodent of fear and shame swept away from her mind, she basked in the light of renewed hope. Luisa squirmed around on her lap to reach up with chubby arms and pull hairpins from her aunt's hair. Teresa kissed the top of her head.

"I likely saw him at his worst. A cowhand on a Saturday night is no saint. Anyway, Pearson will send O'Brien into town to see me as soon as he returns."

"And when will that be?" she asked lightly in an attempt to mask her interest.

"I have no idea."

Luisa slid off Teresa's lap and began to pick up hairpins from the ground to give to her aunt. "Thank you, mi niña. Y gracias a usted, hermano."

"Thanks? For what?" He pulled a cigar from his shirt pocket, a sure sign that he was in a good mood.

"For making the trip and for bringing back such good news." As Luis drew on his cigar, Teresa watched the orange glow swell, just as her dreams expanded at this turn of events. Jack had not ignored her letter; he didn't even know of it. "I'm pleased that Jack appears to be a responsible person in your eyes."

"You are easily pleased then. I still mean to confront him for taking you for a Sunday ride without a proper chaperon. But, Teresa, all may turn out as you wish."

She stood and picked up Luisa to kiss her again, then plopped her on her father's lap.

"You know, Teresa, you look like a young girl with your hair down."

"I still feel like one in some ways."

"You know the saying, 'Eres tan joven como te sientes.'"

"Sí, and tonight I do feel young. Buenas noches, Luis." Teresa was amazed that Luis spoke Spanish to her is if she were a valued customer at the Emporium. She had seldom seen this compassionate, almost tender side of her stepbrother. Feeling hungry, she joined the family in the casa grande; they were just sitting down for supper. Perhaps the load was not too heavy for this beast of burden to carry, she thought.

On Independence Day the peal of San Agustín's bells shattered Teresa's sleep. She had kicked off her sheet in the night, but she was still bathed in sweat. The sound of artillery fire and firecrackers made the day seem hotter still.

After breakfast she saw Luis standing in the shade of the ramada, dressed in his white Volunteer Fire Department uniform. She dipped water from the olla on the porch and joined him, sipping from the tin dipper. "Sounds like everyone is celebrating early."

Luis struggled with the gold buttons on his uniform, and Teresa set the dipper on the bench. "Here, let me do it. So you are marching in the parade this year."

"Don't know why the volunteers picked white. So hard to keep clean." Luis glanced at the sky. "What happened to our rain? San Juan's Day has passed and he brought us none so far."

"No, he hasn't. I hope he doesn't until after the parade. I'll see you at Carrillo's."

Luis donned his tall, wide-brimmed fire helmet. "Doubt that I'll stay after we march. Too many speeches. Too hot."

On Main Street Teresa stood in the meager shade of a young apple tree near Carrillo's Gardens to watch the parade that started at the Military Plaza and would wind up at the gardens. At the head of a dozen mounted Tucsonans, Mayor Fred Maish led the parade, riding a palomino bedecked with a silver ornamented saddle and bridle. On a horse-drawn wagon decorated in red, white, and blue bunting, several women costumed as colonial dames posed in front of a large American flag. Since Fort Lowell had closed earlier that year, their military band had been replaced by Federico Ronstadt's popular brass band, Club Filarmónico. Behind them, Luis, carrying a bright red Fire Department banner, marched beside a fire wagon along with other volunteer fire fighters. Teresa applauded her stepbrother, and he grinned and waved at her.

She was caught up in the crush of spectators following the parade as they funneled through the gates, swelling the crowd already waiting in the gardens. People elbowed one another for a good view of the bunting-festooned podium where Tucson town fathers orated grandly and at length, sweat running down their faces.

When the orations concluded, Teresa wandered about the gardens looking for Mercedes. She found her friend and her mother seated in the shade of a cottonwood tree near the lake.

"Teresa, join us," Mercedes called out.

"Buenas tardes, Señora Mendes." Teresa chatted with the two women for a few minutes before she managed to get Mercedes aside under the ruse of buying lemonade.

"Jack has not been ignoring me. He's been in Mexico. I want so to marry him, but I fear I don't know how to bring it about."

"You either lure him into your trap with a carrot or use a pry bar to prod him into it." Mercedes, her dark eyes sparkling, swished her skirts and waltzed around Teresa.

"I don't know what type he is."

"Hm, I predict he wants to be lured with a carrot." Mercedes put her arm around Teresa and smiled impishly.

After leaving Mercedes and her mother, Teresa started down Simpson Street for home. A sudden whim seizing her, she stopped at the shrine of El Tiradito. On a mound of earth a miniature hut, crudely fashioned from tin, sheltered a few flickering candles. According to legend, this shrine was the grave of a fallen shepherd, who was murdered by a jealous husband. It was believed that if you lit a candle that burned all night, wishes would come true. Though she had none to light, Teresa dropped to her knees on earth blackened and waxy from the drippings of countless candles. She prayed for her romance to go forward. As if in answer, a welcome draft of wind fanned her face, and raindrops spattered the dry earth in Tucson's first summer shower.

Another week had passed, and Jack had neither written nor appeared. Teresa sat at the small table in her bedroom and began another letter to Jack, while Chloe's kittens tried to climb out of the basket on their wobbly legs. Teresa crumpled two sheets of paper before she was satisfied with a third draft. Again she entreated Jack to come to town and meet at the library before he saw Luis.

The next morning Teresa hurried off without breakfast. Shouts of a Papago wood seller on Stone Avenue reminded her that the casita was almost out of wood. Ay dios mío, she thought, last night was there still fire in the kitchen stove when she tossed in the first drafts of her letter? She visualized her hand on the lifter slotted in the round black stove lid. Was the metal hot? No, she and her mother had eaten a cold supper. This morning had Jessie looked inside before chunking in mesquite wood to start a fire for coffee? If she had found the crumpled pages, she no doubt read them. For the rest of the morning Teresa's mood progressed from suspicious unease to outright certainty that Jessie had found those damning sheets of paper.

At noon Teresa slapped on her straw hat and hurried home. The relentless sun ruled a brass sky, seemingly unimpressed by the heavy-bottomed clouds massing over the Santa Rita Mountains to the south. Jessie greeted her, placing plates of tamales, lettuce, cheese, and tomatoes on the kitchen table while she chattered to Teresa. "Well, the judge threw the case out of court."

"The case?"

"Dr. Handy's. He is trying to legally obtain their house. Poor Mary. That's all she has left. He has already shipped the children off to his mother in California. What do you suppose John Handy will try next?" Jessie continued her harangue about the perfidy of men. Teresa answered in monosyllables, knowing from her mother's airiness that she had found the pages and was in one of her cat-and-mouse moods.

After the meal, Jessie smiled and said, "Tess, I'm surprised at you. Writing to a man. A man I don't even know. Who is he? What is this mystery about seeing him at the library?"

"How did you know I wrote to a man?"

"Oh, that's simple. I found some pages of a letter you began, but evidently thought better of. Perhaps you didn't send a letter after all."

"I sent it this morning, though that's scarcely any of your concern."

"Why, Tess, of course I'm concerned about you. Although you are attractive in your way, you are not—I mean, men have not shown the same interest in you as suitors did in Margaret. I am worried about you. At your age, you won't attract a man who seeks you for your good qualities. You seem to be making a great parade over this one; doubtless he's some unprincipled adventurer."

"How dare you call him that? You don't know anything about him or his principles."

Jessie's smile faded. "If he is really your friend, you can tell me about him. Why does Luis want to speak to him? Why must you see him first? You are clearly upset about something. Tell me what's afoot. If you don't, I shall ask Luis."

"You want me to remain an old maid—it's what you've always wanted. Who else would you find to take care of you? Jessie, Mr. O'Brien is attracted to me. He loves me."

"Love!" The word sounded like a snarl on Jessie's lips. Her scar turned crimson. "Has he compromised you?"

"Compromised me? No! He loves me. And I love him." Teresa's conviction surprised her. Voicing her feeling for Jack, the dream of love seemed to have become flesh.

"You know nothing of this so called 'love,' of exchanges between a man and a woman."

Teresa felt the blood rise to her face in a tide of anger she couldn't contain. Rising, she gripped the edge of the table. "You are wrong. I do know of love."

"What do you mean? Has he violated you?"

"No, but I am loved. Don't you even know the difference?" Teresa shouted. "No, I suppose you don't. You never loved Papá—you merely tolerated him."

"You shameless whore! My own flesh and blood. You've undone me. You always have—from the day you were conceived." Her hands on her head, Jessie rushed to her bed, screaming, "The wind, the earthquake, the earth, the fire! You ungrateful child, you viper, the regret of my life. Oh, my head, my head."

Teresa immediately sobered. She had propelled her mother into one of her deranged tirades that always led to a blinding headache. Teresa ran to the casa grande to beg Olivia to send a child to Luis to explain that she must care for Jessie the rest of the afternoon. Socorro returned to the casita with her to help with Jessie, who lay weeping on her bed.

For the next few minutes Jessie alternately screamed or wept softly. When she grew quieter, Socorro tried to soothe her with a cool compress. Jessie threw it on the floor—tin basin, water, and all. But she eventually allowed Socorro to place the cloth on her forehead. Worn down by the violence of her emotions, she fell asleep.

"She seems over the worst of it. What brought it on?" Socorro whispered to her niece.

"Oh, Tía Socorro, she saw pages of my letter to Mr. O'Brien. She can't bear the thought that I have a suitor. She thinks I am her mainstay for the rest of her life. I may be, at that."

Her aunt put her arms around Teresa. "Ah, Palomita, perhaps not. We'll see. I'll go help Luis at the store. You stay here. Perhaps a bit of music will soothe her when she wakes."

In the parlor Teresa picked up her library book. At first, she found it hard to concentrate, but eventually she became curious about the rebellious girl in *The Mill on the Floss*.

After an hour Jessie called from her curtained alcove, "Socorro, bring me some water."

"Socorro's at the Emporium. How do you feel, Jessie?"

"My pain is frightful, thanks to you."

Teresa fetched a glass of water from the olla on the porch. "Would you like to hear some music?"

"No. Leave me alone." Jessie began to sob again.

Ignoring her mother's command, Teresa sat at the piano and played hymn tunes. Long ago she discovered that music soothed her mother when she was in this state.

This day is the 3rd day of April, 1863 ~ Something wonderful happened. We were playing hide and seek and I was on the next street hiding in bushes. I heard music. I went up to the front porch to hear better. A lady came out and got mad at me and yelled whos there then another lady came out She was nice and sed I shuld come in to listen the next day. I did. We had tea in cups with pink flowers and she played some more for me. The piano lady sed she wood give me lessons. I had 10 lesons so far and I am so happy. Jessie likes me to do this.

Jessie called for bread and milk. In the kitchen Teresa tore bread into a tumbler, sprinkled it with sugar, and poured milk over it. In Kansas, Jessie's mother had prepared this concoction for her children when they were afflicted with anything from chicken pox to a fractured bone. Jessie had perpetuated this tradition with her own children. Teresa pulled a kitchen chair to the bed, propped her mother up on pillows, and spooned the soggy mixture into her mouth.

"Milk isn't cold enough," Jessie complained.

"Don't know why. It was right next to the ice."

After a few bites Jessie pushed away the spoon, her mouth turned down in an expression of disgust. "It appears I have never really known you, but I know what you've become."

10 The Dream ❖ July 19

Pleasant childhood images fill Teresa's dream. . . . She and Margarita play beside the acequia, an irrigation canal west of the Presidio wall. A Mexican woman, one hand steadying a basket on her head, comes to wash clothes. The lavandera warns them, "Niñas, don't play here—you might drown."

Clutching their cornhusk dolls, the sisters move inside the crumbling walls of the Presidio, where everything is reassuringly familiar. Adobes have been pilfered, leaving great gaps in the wall. Wagon wheel ruts crosshatch the hard-packed earth. A handful of impoverished families live in the few remaining dwellings huddled against the walls, once quarters for Spanish, then Mexican troops. No green thing grows. Wind-whipped sand sifts over their faces, gritty between their teeth and mummifying their bare feet. A wagon hurtles through the wide opening on the west, and the sisters run to get out of its way. Columns of choking dust whirl about them, bringing tears to their eyes.

The sunlit dream darkens into a nightmare. Teresa wanders alone in the Presidio. An ochre-colored snake of clay and wet mud, as large as a cannon, slithers after her. Terror-stricken, she struggles through powdery dirt, only inches ahead of the snake that follows her and mews loudly. . . .

Teresa awakened, her heart beating wildly, her mouth full of grit. The hot, dry wind that had blown for days had filled her room with dust. Dirt sagged in the cheesecloth attached to the vigas on the ceiling, and some had filtered down on her. She realized the kittens mewing had awakened her. Chloe, who had gone out to the kitchen for food scraps in her dish, returned. The kittens quieted as they latched onto her nipples.

The hot night enclosed Teresa's body, and she pulled her cotton nightgown up and thrashed her legs impatiently. Why hadn't Jack come or even acknowledged her letters? Has the love he professed vanished like a desert mirage? Surely he's back from Mexico by now. Three weeks had passed since Luis brought back his favorable report from Dos Colinas. Waiting for word from Jack was an agony consuming her, tightening her stomach in knots.

As she had feared, Jessie spoke to Luis about her scandalous liaison. When he accosted Teresa about it, she looked him straight in the eye and lied; they had merely gone to San Xavier. She explained that Jessie had spun her own story about the innocent outing. Luis, still in his benevolent frame of mind, believed Teresa. Tía Socorro presented another problem in her life. Worried about her, several times she had mixed up a vile-tasting brew, ephedra tea, and made her niece drink it.

Though it was Sunday, Teresa had no intention of going to church. At dawn she dressed in her riding habit, a brown gabardine suit with a divided skirt, and donned a tan felt hat tied down with a long blue scarf. She tied down her tan felt hat with a long blue scarf. She slipped out the back gate, relieved to escape without being seen by anyone. At the corral on Simpson Street she offered her dappled gray horse a lump of sugar and slipped a bridle over his head. "Pegasus, you want to go flying, don't you?" She threw her side saddle over his back, tightened the cinch, and led him to the corral fence to mount him.

Aiming to follow the Santa Cruz north, she rode toward Sentinel Hill, jogging on the dirt road to a duet of creaking leather and clip-clop of hooves. The dwindling river trickled beside fields of corn, pumpkins, and barley. With so little water to oversee, the sluice gates overseen by the zanjero, the water master, remain closed. A dust devil whirled across fields in a zigzag path, seemingly drawn to horse and rider like a magnet. Sand needled her face, and she jammed her hat down on her head and pulled her scarf over her mouth. Arching his neck, Pegasus sidestepped until he hit the brush fence that kept cattle out of fields. Patting his shoulder and speaking to him, Teresa calmed him.

A few trees at Warner's Mill at the base of Sentinel Peak and the convento orchard offered shade. She decided to stop there and "hitched her horse to the ground" by simply dropping his reins—a feat that Lito had patiently taught her. Dismounting, she rummaged in the saddlebag for her canteen and sipped warm water. Then she took out the sketchbook and pencil she always carried. In the orchard she sat on a rock shaded by an old apple tree to sketch the adobe ruins. Mounds of reeking cow pies attracted swarms of pesky flies, but she suffered them for the welcome shade. Legs folded under them, dark red cattle belonging to Tucson merchant Sam Hughes lay in the shadow of the mission walls.

Although she had sketched the crumbling adobe walls of the convento a half dozen times since her school days, every drawing was different, each marking the progressive deterioration of the hundred-year-old structure, as the adobe walls melted into the earth that had once formed them. Doors and windows—any salvageable wood—had long since disappeared.

Teresa limned in the building's seven arches on the second-story, sketching them as she imagined they once looked. The massive building next to the Franciscans' mission church once housed a school and workshops. Apaches Mansos, seeking protection from their wilder cousins, had helped to construct the buildings. A few of these peaceful Apache families still scratched out a living at the base of Sentinel Peak, crossing the river to barter corn and squash to townspeople for cooking utensils or clothes.

Though she concentrated on perspective, shadows, and textures, eventually images of Jack crept into her mind. She held the drawing at arm's length and frowned, finding it too labored. She packed up her sketchbook and remounted Pegasus. Taking a different route home, she rode east on Mission Lane.

The weather rapidly changing, black clouds now obscured the sun as if a Mexican woman had thrown her dark rebozo over it. The heat still oppressive, the wind that drove grit in her eyes bore the welcome scent of rain. She urged her horse into a trot, turning south on Meyer Street.

A short distance down the street she glanced up. Jack O'Brien stood on the balcony of the Palace Hotel with his arm around a woman. They faced the Santa Rita Mountains where forks of jagged lightning licked the desert like a serpent's tongue.

11 Storm ❖ July 19

Teresa spun Pegasus around, retracing their path and heading south on Main Street. At the Velarde corral on Simpson Street, her horse nervously pranced, sidestepping and shying at blowing leaves and papers. Leaning into the wind, she stowed his saddle and bridle in the shed. Pegasus and the two other Velarde horses whinnied and streaked up and down the corral, nostrils flared, tails and manes flying.

Before Teresa reached home, the storm broke. Lightning shafts split open the blue-black sky, followed by ear-shattering thunder. She ducked into the Emporium's backyard to wait it out. Not having her key to the store, she huddled on the patio bench, its narrow porch offering little protection from wind-driven rain. Sheets of water barraged the tin rooftop, and water spurted from canales, creating a deafening roar.

Nature's violence was no fiercer than the storm raging inside Teresa. Cold fury unleashed, she moaned, am I meant to go through life alone? Has hope been raised—only to be dashed? Jack, why couldn't you have chosen me? Por dios mío, what's to become of me now?

She heard her own scream emerging from the deep well of her existence, the nothingness of her life. The wind echoed her lament. When the rain slackened, she slowly moved toward home, sloshing in water above her ankles. The Velarde midday meal long past, she would have no one to face except Jessie.

To Teresa's surprise, Tía Socorro met her at the door of the casita. "¡Nombre de Dios! You weren't here for dinner. Where have you been, Palomita? We feared you were washed away."

"Lo siento. I was coming home, but I got only as far as the Emporium."

Teresa stepped inside. The casita's roof was leaking badly and Socorro had placed pots and kettles around to catch drips. The sound of the storm outside was syncopated by the steady plink-plonk of drops in the house in varying tones of the scale.

Socorro said in a low voice, "Your mother is feeling worse. I came to sit with her. Pobrecita, you are soaked through. Ven, quitate esa ropa mojada."

While Socorro fetched rags to mop up puddles Teresa had made, she removed her boots and crossed the carpet to part the curtain around her mother's bed. "Tía Socorro says you aren't feeling well."

"Tess, you never think about the worry you give me," Jessie rasped in her sickbed voice.

"I couldn't make it back before the storm broke. I'm sorry I worried you."

"You have been the worry of my life. Fire . . . wind . . . earth . . . water . . . you are my certain damnation! Leave me alone." Jessie began to sob.

Teresa let the curtain around her mother's bed fall back.

When Socorro returned, she asked what had upset Jessie. Teresa shrugged, took the rags and started wiping up the floor.

"Luis left for the store just before you came. Afraid of flooding," Socorro said.

"Somehow we missed each other in the storm. It's already flooding there. I'll go help him."

"Palomita, you shouldn't go out in this rain again. You'll come down with the ague. But if you are determined, at least get into dry clothing, Teresa," Socorro insisted.

"¿Para qué? It's still raining."

"Teresita, go change."

As she slipped into dry clothes, Teresa thought, prolong this moment. All these moments, pray God. Anything to postpone the time when the vision of Jack and that woman on the balcony returned to haunt her. It would fix on her weary brain and she'd have no rest.

When she returned to the parlor, Socorro said, "Take Hector's old slicker."

Teresa shuffled music from the top of a wooden chest next to the piano. Musty odors of old garments mingled with the violet sachet tucked inside. She pulled out the slicker—her father called the raincoat a "fish"—and its sharp odor sparked the memory of a wet ride with him: she perched behind him on his horse, her arms around him, her nose jammed against his slicker, comforted by the assurance of a father's strength and protection.

Wrapped in his long raincoat, Teresa hurried back to the store. Luis had lit gaslights and heaped goods from lower shelves to countertops. She emptied the lowest file drawers in her office and then returned to help him. The muddy water inside the building, already several inches high, was rising rapidly. Luis went out to channel water away from the back door with a shovel. Teresa found gunnysacks in the storage shed to wedge against the front door.

When Luis and Teresa had done all they could, they peered out the back door, listening to rain hammer the tin roof and gush from the canales. Standing shoulder to shoulder with him, Teresa thought of Maggie and Tom in *The Mill on the Floss*, brother and sister drowning in a flood, reunited after years of disagreement. Perhaps this flood would bring harmony to her and Luis—but in life, not death. Then she bitterly reminded herself, it was not the love of a brother that she desperately sought.

"Thanks for coming, Teresa. The rain has slackened now. Unless it's worse, we'll get through this. Teresa, you look worn out. Aren't you feeling well?"

"I found out . . . word has come to me that I am nothing to Mr. O'Brien. What I hoped for will never come to be. Luis, I want to make a new life. Maybe go to California. Maybe go to an art school." Teresa turned to face her brother. "Luis, would you give me back the money I have invested in the Emporium?"

"I'm sorry about O'Brien. But California? Art school? What are you thinking? That would take far more than you have in the business." Turning away from the doorway, he lifted his hands, palms up. "You know how hard it has been to build this. Yes, we have a nest egg now, but I need it. I plan to build an addition in the back. I must borrow to do it. Ah, Teresa, the Velarde name is at last coming to mean something in this town. Don't you understand?"

"Of course I understand. I am also a Velarde."

Luis looked at her, a strange gleam in his eyes. "No, Teresa, you are not truly a Velarde. Not even half, as you think."

"What do you mean?"

"Jessie was—was with child when my father married her."

"No. It's impossible. You made this up. You've always despised Jessie and me."

"I don't despise either of you. I've always taken care of you."

"Oh, you've certainly done your duty. That doesn't mean you love us."

"Love? Chihui, I have done a great deal for a stepmother who shows me so little love. But when I said you are not a Velarde, I was speaking the truth. Your mother was attacked and raped by an Apache in a raid. When I was just a boy, Father made me promise never to tell anyone. Teresa, I'm sorry, but it's time you knew."

"No, no, no! It cannot be." Teresa shouted as she sloshed across the patio in slanting rain. "I'll ask Jessie. She will tell me the truth. Papá *was* my father too. I know he was."

As Teresa neared the back gate to the casita, unearthly screams filled the air. An apparition in white hurtled past her in the dark. Socorro burst through the back gate in pursuit. "Espérate, ven, ven!"

Teresa caught her aunt by the arm. "¿Que pasa?"

"¡Tu mamá! We must stop her! ¡Está delirante!"

"She's delirious? Go back to the house. Bring a lantern. I'll go after her."

As she followed her mother, Teresa shouted, "Jessie, stop! Please wait for me."

Rushing water made footing treacherous, and she slowed to a walk. At the next street she paused, wondering if Jessie went right or left. She caught a glimpse of a white figure heading west, but it soon vanished.

At Main Street she heard a muffled cry coming from the direction of Carrillo's Gardens. Her mother was now heading north. As wary as a wild animal, she seemed to dart willy-nilly in any direction. Teresa rushed to the garden and along its central path. A wavering voice, singing tunelessly, guided her to the lake.

Teresa redoubled her speed, only to slip and fall in knee-deep water. The lake had overflowed! Without moon or stars, the night was black. How could she avoid the rock-lined paths, shrubs and trees? She screamed for help, "¡Auxcilio!"

Then Teresa saw a flash of white ahead; it was her mother caught in the glow of light. She turned back to see Tía Socorro, her features lit by the lantern she carried. Teresa shouted again, "¡Ayude! dios mio!"

She threw herself into chin-deep water to seize her mother. Jessie thrashed and flailed against her with the prodigious strength of the demented. Teresa subdued her and dragged her toward the light on shore.

Socorro hallooed, swinging the lantern. Rain-slanted light revealed Luis at her side. He lunged through the water with Socorro following. He took Jessie's limp body, and Teresa blindly plunged forward after him until sharp pain streaked up her legs. She fell over the embankment, regained her feet, and threw her arms around a tree, the rough bark pressed against her cheek.

12 Truth or Lies? ❖ July 20 to 22

Sunlight streamed through a crack in the muslin curtains, casting a bright stripe on the bed. Socorro gently pressed Teresa's shoulder. "¿Estás despierta, querida?"

"Ay, Tía Socorro, I'm awake now." Teresa's head swiveled away from the window. "I've been trying to wake up for some time, but I keep falling back to sleep and dreaming I'm a little girl."

"They must have been pleasant dreams—you had a smile on your face. I've been in a half dozen times, but I didn't waken you. You needed your sleep. What you did was very brave, Palomita. Eres una mujer valiente. Le salvaste la vida a tu mamá."

"Is Jessie all right?"

"I think so. She's still asleep. A wonder she didn't drown. She swallowed so much water."

"No me acuerdo. I don't even remember how I got home."

"It took all my might to pull you from that tree. You were holding on for dear life. But you walked home leaning on me. Your poor shins. You must have fallen somewhere. I've dressed them. Bad scrapes."

Teresa gingerly touched her legs and the pain brought back the memory of the night before. Tía Socorro had helped her into bed and bandaged the scrapes on her shins before she brewed some mesquite bark tea to keep fever away.

"Jessie wandered in circles. How did you ever find us?" Teresa asked.

"Before she ran out into the storm, she had been ranting about finding a boat to save her from the flood. I thought she might go to the gardens for a boat. Luis came home soon after you did. So we went straight to Carrillo's."

"Good thinking, Tía." Teresa turned to the window again. "Tanta lluvia. And yet the sun shines this morning."

"Are you hungry, Palomita? Estoy haciendo tortillas. Before I made the tortillas I had to strain ants out of the lard. The water brings them in. I also made chicken soup."

Two of Chloe's black kittens clawed up the coverlet onto the bed. Teresa stroked them. After breakfast, Socorro went to help at the Emporium, and Teresa sat with Jessie. She seemed in retreat from the world, either dozing or staring at the ceiling. While her mother slept, Teresa sat in the parlor, her head spinning with the vision of her topsy-turvy world. Nothing was the same.

Jessie had clearly been out of her mind. She had long feared the four elements that she declared were destroying her life. How ironic that the overflowing lake had drawn her to it like a siren calling.

Teresa was also haunted by the horror Luis had revealed about her birth. She couldn't believe that she wasn't Hector Velarde's daughter. Why, all her life she had been told she looked like him, a comparison that always pleased her. Now to be called half Apache had sent her reeling. Que desgracia. It was too terrible to think about. As she envisioned the scene on the hotel balcony, she descended into a dark whirlwind of despair. It would have been better had she drowned along with her mother.

Teresa shuffled into the kitchen to stoke the stove with wood and heat the chicken soup, but at Jessie's bedside she failed to tempt her to swallow any. She could eat none herself. Continually nodding off, Teresa finally stretched out on her own bed. In the afternoon Socorro awakened her from a suffocating and dreamless sleep.

"Tía Socorro, is Jessie better?"

"Her eyes are open, but I can't say she's any better. Come judge for yourself, Palomita."

In the parlor Teresa pulled aside the curtain around her mother's bed. Lusterless in her wan face, Jessie's eyes remained focused on the ceiling. Teresa rubbed her mother's hand. "¿Tía, que le pasa? What is wrong with her? She's never been like this before."

"Shh!" Socorro whispered, leading Teresa into the kitchen. "Be careful when you speak in front of her. She may not be able to utter a word, but she most likely can hear you."

◆ ◆ ◆

The next day a merciless sun blasted the sodden earth. Though afternoon clouds obscured the mountains, no rain fell in town. After supper Teresa and Socorro surveyed the ruined garden, their feet crackling on a patchwork of drying mud cakes. Tomato and squash plants had washed away in the flood, and corn stalks drooped. The two women talked quietly in the ramada. "Would you tell me about Jessie when you first knew her?"

"I met your mother when Hector asked me to come up from Sonora to Tucson to help her. Luis was two or so and you were just a baby. I stayed for about a year. Then I came back again when Margarita was born."

"And Hector was truly my father?"

"Sí, claro que si." Socorro turned to her. "Why do you ask?"

Teresa was silent for a moment. "Luis told me Hector wasn't really my father."

"Que tontería. What nonsense! Luis is mistaken. Of course you're his child. You look just like him. Hector would have told me if you weren't. Jessie always spoke of him as your father."

Teresa thought, so Luis had lied to her! Why? Just to hurt her? After a moment she asked, "Tía, you told me that I was born in Tubaca, but you didn't tell me why Jessie lived there. I know she came from Kansas."

"Let me think. . . Hector once told me the story. In Kansas Jessie was orphaned when she was young. She lived with her grandparents. When they died, a neighboring family was moving west, and they agreed to take her to California. She had a sister there. But when they reached Arizona, she became ill and couldn't go on with them. A ranch family near Tubaca took her in."

"How difficult that must have been for Jessie. How did she meet my father?"

"After Hector mustered out of the army, he worked on a ranch near Tubaca. He married a girl named Manuela, and she died giving birth to Luis. Then Hector married your mother. She was only seventeen, y muy bonita, and my brother fell in love with her."

"Why did they move to Tucson?"

"Hector told me your mother was unhappy in Tubaca. She begged to move away."

"I wonder why I was never told about this," Teresa said. "Jessie never talks about those days in Tubaca, though she loves to tell stories about Kansas. . . How did she get those burns?"

Socorro shook her head. "Hector thought she probably was burned in a fire in Kansas, but she wouldn't talk about it. All these years it has remained a secret."

Tears welled up in Teresa's eyes. What terrible tragedy had befallen her mother?

Socorro took Teresa's hand. "As long as I've known her, your mother has suffered from melancholía. Seems part of her nature. Bad moods would come, and I would take care of her."

"You must have loved her even then."

"Love Jessie? I don't know if I ever loved her, Palomita. I felt compassion for her, but you and Luis and little Margarita were the ones I loved. Ustedes son quien yo considero como mi familia."

Teresa embraced Socorro. "I know how you loved us. But you are always so kind to Jessie that I thought that you loved her as well."

"I don't love her, no, but at last I've forgiven her."

"Forgiven her? ¿Y que hay que perdonar?"

"For killing my brother. She killed him with her cold heart. He drank himself to death because of her."

"¡Socorro! ¡Pero los Apaches lo mataron!"

"No, he died of mescal."

"But he went with the men who raided the Arivaipa Apaches on the San Pedro River. I've heard the story many times."

"Your father started out with the party—Juan Elías and a few others from Tucson. And many Papagos. But Hector was full of drink and fell off his horse near Cebadillo Pass. His friend, Enrique Portillo, put him back on his horse. But he fell off again, so Enrique thought it best to leave him there to sleep it off. When Enrique returned after the Apache raid, vultures were circling at the pass. He rode off to have a look. Era tu padre."

"Socorro, no. No puede ser la verdad esso. It can't be."

"What I tell you is God's truth, Palomita. Enrique said it looked like mí hermano had stumbled off a cliff and fallen to his death. Thank God, Enrique was alone then. He brought Hector's body to us. He was so ashamed he had left him there. He told the story only to your mother and me. No one else knew." Socorro pulled a handkerchief from her apron pocket and dabbed at her eyes.

"Oh, Tía Socorro, I can't bear it. I'm glad I never knew."

Socorro wrapped her arms around her niece. "Your mother and I made up the story of the brave Apache fighter. We buried him as a hero."

"Some people in Tucson said there was nothing heroic about the raid. The Apache warriors were gone when the Papagos and Americanos arrived. They ended up killing Apaches all right, but mostly women and children. Many called it a massacre. Some still do."

"Pues yo no, I don't. Essos demonios Apaches have killed our women and children without mercy, sin misericordia," Socorro said bitterly.

Teresa's spirits sagged. In the past few hours she had lost and regained a father; now his image was shattered. "It must have been terrible to find out your brother died that way. How did Jessie take it?"

Socorro covered her face with her hands and cried. "I suspect she was relieved. . . Oh Palomita, she never allowed Hector in her bed after Margarita was born. And she constantly ridiculed him. After my brother's death, I raged at her for breaking his heart. For killing him. I fear my anger marked her; it seared her soul. In time I forgave her for what she did to my brother, but I've never forgiven myself for what I did to Jessie."

"Jessie and Papá quarreled, but I never knew you had differences with her."

"In time we made up."

"You are a talented actress. For as long as I can remember, Jessie appeared to love you."

The two women sat together quietly, each lost in memories.

13 Reginald Multaney ❖ July 24

Clank … turn … stop … clank … turn … stop.

Teresa sat in a chair by her mother's bed in an upstairs ward at St. Mary's Hospital. She sketched the windmill outside, its sound a metallic echo of Jessie's struggle to breathe. If only my mother had such a wheel to draw breath into her lungs, she thought.

Two days after her ordeal in the lake, Jessie had turned feverish, her breath labored. Olivia made a manda—a vow to the Virgin Mary to pray at church each morning at dawn. Socorro told Olivia to go right ahead with her manda. She herself was praying, but she was calling in la curandera, Doña Tiburcia, the neighborhood healer.

The next morning the old Mexican woman with her bag of herbs had hobbled in, leaning on her cane. She made mesquite bark tea for Jessie's fever, added a secret herb, and spooned it into Jessie's mouth. Next she rubbed lard mixed with kerosene and another special herb on her patient's chest.

Noticeably better the next morning, Jessie suffered a relapse that afternoon. Chiding herself for waiting so long, Teresa sent for Dr. Handy. After he examined Jessie, he diagnosed pneumonia and arranged to admit her to St. Mary's Hospital.

Nuns fluttered around tending to patients in the sunny ward that was only partially full. Teresa closed her sketchbook, setting it on the windowsill. She turned Jessie over and pulled up her nightgown to rub her back with Electric Oil, a home remedy Jessie's mother had used. Dr. Handy said the oil could do no harm. Though it might possess no medicinal powers, Teresa hoped that the familiar acrid smell would comfort her mother. When she finished, she turned Jessie onto her back again and fussed with the bedclothes. Silent, except for her troubled breathing—a kind of grunt—Jessie lay on the hospital bed with her eyes closed.

Teresa grasped her mother's hand and murmured, "Dear God, be merciful; let her live, let her live long enough to know some happiness in her life of disappointment."

Jessie's eyes opened.

"Do you hear me, Jessie? I'm so sorry about all the suffering life has brought you. I don't know what terrible things have happened to you, but from now on I'll try to bring you some joy, some happiness. Get well soon and come home. Can you hear me? Jessie, please speak to me."

Her mother turned her head and looked into Teresa's eyes, her cold fingers tightening on her daughter's hand. A wisp of a smile appeared on her lips before she closed her eyes again.

"Jessie, please say something, I beg of you." Teresa squeezed her mother's hand, but received no answering pressure this time. Her eyes barely focused, Teresa stared through teardrop prisms at dust motes floating in the sunlight shafting across the bed's coverlet.

For the rest of the morning Teresa sat beside Jessie and occasionally addressed her; she failed to elicit a response. Left alone with dismal thoughts, Teresa dozed off now and then. A shifting phantasm of her father's death, of her mother's murky secret, of her own origin, loomed up with nightmarish enormity, frightening her awake.

She threw off her muzziness and clearheadedly attacked the specters one by one. How could Tía Socorro be certain that I was Hector's child? My aunt wasn't acquainted with Jessie until she came to Tucson. Socorro's tale of Jessie's unhappiness as a young married woman seems to authenticate Luis's story about my parentage. Did an Apache force himself upon my mother? Was that the secret Socorro calculated Jessie never revealed? Oh God, am I, Teresa Velarde, half Apache, and not a Velarde at all? How can I verify this story?

For distraction she pulled *The Mill on the Floss* from her satchel, noting it was due several days ago. Though she had finished it, she reread its final pages, pondering the strange, sad relationship between brother and sister. She closed the book, wryly thinking: the flood on the River Floss resolved poor Maggie's terrible problems. The Santa Cruz should have swallowed her, Teresa, and resolved hers. Choked with misery, she fell asleep again.

◆ ◆ ◆

That afternoon Socorro, Olivia, and Manuela visited. "So, Manuela, you managed to take off your apron for a little while." Teresa hugged her.

Manuela smiled. Her sharp nose and chin, and bright black eyes imbued her with the look of a nestling awaiting food. "Just for a little while, Tía Teresa."

Teresa rested her hand lightly on her niece's shoulder then caught her breath and shuddered. Would she be horrified if she knew her aunt was half Apache?

Socorro stepped to the bed, kissed Jessie's cheek and took her hand. "¿Como está?"

"Her breathing's no better. Oh, when will she ever regain her senses?" Teresa cried out.

"Ah, Palomita, you are overwrought. You go on home now."

"I need to go to the Emporium. Luis is all alone," Teresa said with a frown.

"No, he closed the store and is coming here. Teresita, you go on home as I told you. Lito has our wagon out in the back."

Teresa didn't go home. She asked Lito to drop her off at the *Star* office on Congress Street. In the newspaper's files she hoped to find stories of Apache raids that took place in the year of her birth. She was disappointed when the clerk at the counter informed her they had no newspapers in their files as far back as 1854.

"Young woman, what information are you seeking? Perhaps I can be of help," a gravelly voice called out.

At a desk in a dark corner of the room, Teresa saw an open newspaper, smoke spiraling above it. A bald, grizzled-bearded man lowered the pages and tapped cigar ashes on the floor. His suit coat was draped over the back of his swivel chair, his vest food-stained. Arm clips gathered up his shirtsleeves. Balls of string, papers, pencils, and books littered his desk, jumbled together like a pack rat collection.

"I'm looking for stories of Apache attacks near Tubaca in 1854," Teresa answered.

"Ah, you're in luck, young lady. I lived in Tubaca for several years, including the year of 18 and 54. Yours truly was reporting news even then. I can tell you many a story about the raids of those filthy Apaches. In my files at home I have my own handwritten accounts of those days."

"Would it be possible to see them?"

"Your vision appears to be normal. I expect you can." The old man chortled.

"I mean, would you allow me to see them?"

"Certainly. Come back tomorrow. My filing system being what it is, it'll take me awhile to lay my hands on the information you seek."

"I'll gladly pay you for your time."

"No, no, young lady. I expect no compensation. Now let me write down that date. Never trust matters of importance to memory, especially mine. It was 1852, wasn't it?"

"1854, sir."

"Ah yes, the year the U. S. Senate ratified the Gadsden Purchase. That will fix it in my memory."

The old man scribbled on a scrap of paper and slowly got to his feet. "I no longer contribute much in the way of the written word. Merely an ornament here, tolerated because of my many years on this splendid organ for the dissemination of news. Sometimes proffer advice garnered from my vast store of experience." His chuckle led to a prolonged bout of coughing before he extended his hand. "I'm Reginald Multaney. And you are?"

"Teresa Velarde."

"Ah, one of the Velardes. Related to Luis?"

"Yes, his sister." His stepsister, she silently amended, even if I find we don't share the same father.

He scratched his bald pate and grinned. "Happy to meet you, Miss Velarde. Upon occasion your esteemed brother and I are opponents in a game of chance in some of Congress Street's gaming venues."

Teresa thanked him and arranged to visit the newspaper office the following afternoon.

The next evening Teresa fed Chloe, although she could eat nothing herself. She sat in the parlor until nightfall, trying to make sense of what she had learned from the old reporter. Finally, her head in a whirl, she retreated to her bedroom and started to slide the wedge under the door before she realized her mother would not interrupt her. She threw herself on her bed and sobbed until she fell asleep.

Around midnight, Chloe woke her by licking her cheek. The kittens mewed shrilly for their mother. Teresa put Chloe back in her basket and they fastened on to her teats in contentment. From under the bed Teresa pulled out her current journal and sat at her bedside table. Her pen hovered over a page for several minutes before she dipped it in ink and wrote.

July 25, 1891 ~ I've not recorded the entire truth on these pages. I now set down the events which will transform my life from this day forth.

First, Dr. Handy has told us Jessie has pneumonia. There's little hope for she has no will to live.

Second, this afternoon I met with Mr. Reginald Multaney at the paper. He resided in Tubaca for some yrs. & remembers someth an event that happened the year I was born. Four men maskeraded as Apaches to steal cattle at a Tubaca ranch & one of them took violated a young girl there. Mr. Multaney didn't know her name, but he knew the men. Dan White, Perry Archibald, Eduardo Harrington and Spike O'Brien! *The raid took place in early March of 1864 & I was born November 3! The very place, the very time. What damning proof!*

Third, I believe that Mr. Jack O'Brien is Spike O'Brien. That this wretched man is both my *father and my former suitor. I am maddened by the thought of at first I meant to end my life but now I am consumed with anger this despicable man took me in his arms as a lover, not a father. I shall kill him yes, I have no more doubt about of why he came here. To find a daughter, not a niece! Let him deny it I shall not believe him. After I shoot him I will decide what to do with my life I may end it by—I don't know—somehow. Let this be the record of my reasons.*

Teresa blotted the ink stains and set her pen down on her open journal. Fully clothed, she lay on her bed.

14 Dos Colinas ❖ July 26

To top off the load of wood in the wagon Jack whacked a few dead mesquite limbs with the broadside of his ax, knocking them to the ground.

His boss at the ranch, decent to all his cowpunchers, had been especially kind to Jack. Sending him to buy cattle in Mexico was a step up in the world for him. And his boss was pretty understanding when this bout of grippe came along. That laid him up in the bunkhouse with a high fever for a few days. He sure wasn't in shape to run around chasing a snorty steer through brush and cactus. But today, feeling much better, he agreed to bring in a wagonload of wood for old María. Tomorrow he'd be back in the saddle busting his ass with the other cowpunchers.

His boss had upped his pay, and that brought him a mite closer to his dream of owning his own spread. But if he found a certain woman Ned had asked him to locate before he died, he would come into a good bit of money. So far he'd not found her, but the search itself had been rewarding. Three of the four ladies he palavered with were most obliging with their favors. Teresa hadn't been the woman he was looking for, and for some reason he'd not had his way with her. But one of these days he would look her up again. That lady had certain charms the others lacked.

He snaked the fallen branches to the wagon and heaved about half of them into the bed when he had to stop to rest. Damn, he was blowing like a wind-broke horse. Good thing his workday was over; it had begun to sprinkle. When he delivered the wagonload of mesquite to María, he'd have some of her warm grub. She'd make him wash it down with her mesquite bark tea—though he'd beg for a cup of her good strong java—pointing out he no longer had a fever. Then he'd have a good siesta and listen to the rain pounding on the bunkhouse roof.

Jack glanced at the sky to see a jagged fork of lightning, followed by the sound of thunder; he must hurry. A man sitting on a wagon on that high ground up by the ranch house made a mighty fine target for a lightning bolt. Slanting rain poured down.

When he reached the wagon with his last load of wood, he saw a woman in a straw hat walking toward him, leading a horse and brushing wet limbs aside.

Before dawn Teresa had collected the small caliber Winchester rifle and cartridges kept behind the safe at the Emporium before she headed for the corral. The derringer she always carried in her saddlebag would be better at close range, but she didn't intend to get too close to Jack. If only she could drag a cannon along, she'd lob a cannonball at him from a good distance.

Dressed in her gabardine riding habit, neck scarf, and hat, she rode astride her dapple gray horse on a man's saddle at a slow jog. She went south on the old stagecoach road along the Santa Cruz River. At the bridge, her horse nervously pranced and sidestepped across the planks, frightened more by the hollow drum roll of his hooves than by the rushing water below.

Pegasus was still agitated long after they crossed the bridge, and Teresa realized that her shaking hands, shallow breath, and rapid heartbeat was affecting him. She took a deep breath and spoke calmly to him. She realized that her words and patting his sun-warmed hide improved both their spirits.

The Santa Cruz valley, green and grassy from the recent rains, widened as she went south. White wispy mare's tails spanned the sky, with more serious gray mounds of clouds building up behind the Santa Rita and the Rincon Mountains. Bone-weary by midmorning, she turned off the main road, picking her way up an arroyo where a small stream flowed. She dismounted so that Pegasus could drink, taking care that he didn't drink too much. While she listened to him snort and slurp, she removed her jacket, drank from her canteen, and fanned her face with her straw hat.

Weeks ago, when the idea to make a trip to Dos Colinas had first occurred to her, she had asked Lito the best way to reach it. He told her, "On the old road before you see the white towers of the Mission

San Xavier, look for an old windmill and the ruins of an adobe ranch house. From that place you ride the length of a cornfield and you will find the road to Rancho Dos Colinas. All of these things are on the side of the setting sun."

He also warned her she must not ride alone. She promised him she'd ask Luis to accompany her. The old Indian still regarded her with suspicion. "Señor Luis knows the way."

Teresa regretted her lies to her friend Lito. She was nervous. At the sight of the first rider on the road—a poor Mexican farmer by the look of his clothes—she pulled her rifle from its scabbard and carried it across the saddle in front of her. For the next encounters with travelers she repeated this maneuver. In late morning a stage-coach bound for Tucson hurtled by, stirring up choking dust. The sight of a few ranch houses lent her courage, but she was glad she had a rifle and knew how to use it.

November 1, 1884 ~ Luis and Lito took me rabbit hunting yesterday. We started at dawn & rode over rough country towards the Santa Catalinas. I always missed the rabbit. Lito said I must practice to improve my skill in hitting a moving animal. I said I don't like to shoot an innocent creature. He said you must respect the animal & not kill it for sport. The rabbits he took that day would feed his family, & he would thank God for supplying him with food.

By midday, as thunderheads began to build up in the sky, a windmill and adobe ruin came into view, just as Lito had described. "Oh, Pegasus, we've done it! That must be Dos Colinas up there." She turned west on a wagon road. Her stomach knotted and her mouth dry, she rehearsed the story she'd use if she met anyone before she found Jack. She had news for Jack O'Brien, news of the relative he was seeking. That was God's truth.

The ranch, which was indeed spread across two hills—actually mere gentle rises with flat tops—consisted of adobe buildings enclosed by barbed wire fencing. Green ocotillo stakes intertwined with the wire spanning the front had taken root. Branded across the top plank of the gate were the words "Rancho Dos Colinas." A large barn and some corrals stood on the second rise. Several horses stood hip-shot, lifting their heads to gaze at the intruders.

Three mongrels dashed forward, barking and snarling. Calming her horse, Teresa dismounted to open the gate. She shouted at the dogs, and they slunk away. A few chickens that were settled in dust bowls scratched out in the shade of an outbuilding cackled and fluttered off. Her hallooing at the front door of the ranch house went unanswered. In the back yard she allowed Pegasus a pull at the watering trough beneath a clattering windmill, while she sipped from her canteen, the water hot and metallic on her tongue. A door squeaked open, and Teresa whirled around. A short, rotund Mexican woman wearing a blue and white flour sack apron over her black dress filled the doorway.

Teresa approached her, Pegasus in tow. "Buenos días, señora. Busco a Señor O'Brien."

The woman's frown was replaced by a beaming smile as she told Teresa that he was cutting wood by the river. Señor Pearson and the rest were out today. The old woman, gracious as most of her nationality, introduced herself as María, and insisted that her visitor come in for a meal. Far from hungry, Teresa felt obliged to accept. After all, she reasoned, she had pushed her horse hard all morning and it would be wise to rest him before they started back to Tucson.

As they ate beans and tortillas, María chattered with the rapidity of a lonely soul making the most of companionship, her monologue mostly about Señor O'Brien. In answer to the pointed question about why she was seeking him, Teresa responded with her tale about Jack's cousin who had recently come to Tucson on the train but was too ill to ride here.

The old woman's eyes narrowed, reflecting a look that Teresa attributed either to disbelief or disappointment. Perhaps she had hoped for a romance. Sorry, Teresa thought, that is a fairy tale that will never come true. Would to God that it had.

After thanking the woman for her hospitality, Teresa took her leave. While she was inside, it had begun to rain.

Rain dripped from Teresa's straw hat as she rode down the hill. Wagon tracks, now muddied, crossed the road where she had turned off earlier; she wondered why she failed to notice them. She followed the tracks to the river. She made out a figure in the heart of a mesquite bosque—so similar to that of the picnic with Jack that she nearly cried out. Shaking and scarcely breathing, she dismounted and walked forward, leading her horse.

On the other side of a wagon loaded with wood, she saw Jack. Shirtless, his pale skin glistened in the rain. Gulping air to calm herself, Teresa dropped Pegasus's reins and slipped the rifle from its scabbard.

"Well, I'll be. Look who's here. Teresa! Buenos días," Jack called out with a big grin. "What a surprise! Just thinking of you. Did you bring a picnic today?"

"I brought no picnic today."

"¿Que pasa? Something wrong?"

"Wrong?" Teresa cried. "You are what is wrong. You and all your sweet talk."

"Teresa, esperese." Moving toward her, he said, "You don't want to fool around with a rifle like that! Put it down and let's talk. Let's you and me be friends."

"Friends!" she growled. "At one time I had high hopes for your friendship. All summer I've been waiting for it to commence, for you to come visit me. But you have too many other lady friends to romance to find time for me."

"Why are you on the prod? Tranquila, Teresa—"

"I am calm, perfectly calm. Jack, do you remember your words of love by the river? Words you clearly didn't mean. You never came to see me. But that's not the reason I am going to kill you. It's because of what you did to my mother! Because of you she has known a life of misery. You shameless villain—you, you bastard, you are my father!"

"Bullshit! I am not your father!" Jack took his wet shirt from the wagon bench and slipped it on. "Why can't we talk like friends?"

Teresa raised the rifle to her shoulder. "Stay where you are."

"For the love of God, Teresa, put down that rifle!" Two metallic clicks rang out as she chambered a cartridge. Then she fired. For a split second he stared at her, his mouth open in surprise. His unbuttoned shirt flapping, he lunged forward as she fired a second time.

15 Arroyos ❖ July 26

Raindrops pattered on her rifle as Teresa lowered it. Jack fell face down to the ground. At the sight of blood blossoming from the back of his shirt, Teresa cried out, "¡Por Dios!"

Jack struggled to his knees, cursing when he found he couldn't get up.

Teresa's anger suddenly melted. She dropped the rifle and rushed forward to slip her arm around his waist. "Venga, let me help you. Can you climb up to the wagon? I'll drive you back to the ranch."

"No, you bitch, not the ranch, to Tucson. I'm gut shot," Jack yelled, clutching the left side of his abdomen with one hand.

"Jack, no!"

Leaning on her, Jack stumbled to the wagon and sagged against it. With strength born of desperation she dragged the wet branches from the wagon bed. In pelting rain she helped Jack climb up, tore off his bloody shirt, and, using her teeth, ripped it into strips to make compresses. She placed one on his shoulder and bound it with her scarf. Loosening his belt, she spread another compress on his abdomen. Next, she untied the slicker from the back of her saddle, and spread it over him. She grabbed the rifle, and with Pegasus tied behind the wagon, they started for Tucson.

Hoping to arrive before dark, she clenched her teeth as she lashed the horse's rump. Every few miles she stopped to check on Jack, worry gnawing at her because of the precious minutes lost. Moaning in pain, Jack cursed each time she shook him to see if he was conscious. Her ambivalence towards Jack nonplused her. Didn't she hate this man who had ruined her mother's life and toyed with her? Why then was she hell-bent on saving his miserable hide? Her stomach churned as though it held a den of rattlers.

After they had traveled a few miles in the steady downpour, arroyos began to run high. Teresa urged the frightened animal through the first. But the wagon nearly overturned at the next arroyo, wide but deceptively deep, and they barely made it across. At the next, her heart pounding fearfully, she pondered what to do. The water in the arroyo thundered over rocks, sweeping brush and small trees in its swift downhill course.

"Jack!" she shouted, turning in her seat. "Do you know another way to go? We'll drown if we cross here."

"Find out how deep it is. Too damn deep, go upstream and cross," he grunted.

"How do I find out?"

"Tie a rope to the wagon and wade out. I got one under the seat."

Teresa was terrified of the arroyo's raging water. But she was also afraid to leave the road to head upstream. In the deepening gloom they would surely lose their way or tumble into a gully. Though Jack's idea was perilous, she'd have to try it. Making certain the brake was set, she placed large rocks against the wheels. She cinched one end of the rope around the axle of the wagon, the other about her waist, carrying the rest coiled over one arm. She fearfully waded into the torrent. The rushing water immediately pulled her down and carried her bumping along the sandy bed over rocks and tree roots. The rope played out with a jerk. She scrambled to her feet and inched back to the cart along the rope, hand over hand.

"Too fast here. Upstream we'll get lost," she shouted to Jack. "Have to wait."

He cursed her. "Get me to the hospital, you bitch. I'm bleeding to death."

"We'll both drown if I try to cross." She untied the rope and threw it in the cart. As she inspected his wounds in the last light of day, she could see no new bleeding. "You aren't bleeding to death, Jack. It's stopped."

In sopping clothes, her hat lost in the wild ride in the arroyo, and her arms scratched and bruised, Teresa huddled on the wagon seat to wait. In a chink under the black curtain of clouds, the sun's dying glow cast a red pall over the sodden desert and silhouetted the dark mountain peaks in the west. A strident chorus of frogs croaking over the roar of the torrent heightened her panic. It was a lonely and cheerless sound, and she trembled from cold and fear.

July 7, 1864 ~ It is raining and raining I hear so many frogs They get in the ponds of rainwater I am scared of them. Lito told me a story about how the frog gets the rain to come down. His people tie a great big frog up to a tree and it brings the rain. then they may have to untie it to make the rain stop. Poor frog.

When the rushing water subsided a little, Teresa led the wagon horse across the arroyo, comforted Pegasus, still tied on behind, and wearily pulled herself up to the wagon bench. That arroyo proved to be the last one of any size, but the road to Tucson seemed endless. Jack, though still breathing, had lost consciousness; she made no more stops to check on him. The rain stopped and a quarter moon shone between lingering clouds.

At the edge of town they passed a few dark houses where dogs barked at them. She heaved a sigh when a few lighted windows at St. Mary's beckoned them. At the hospital steps she turned around to awaken Jack. "We're at St. Mary's, Jack. Thank God, we're here."

Jack moaned, opened his eyes, and shut them again.

16 St. Mary's ❖ July 27

A smiling beanstalk of a woman came up to Jack's bed with a tray of food.

"Awake now? Good morning. And how are we feeling today? Dr. Handy says you should have good nourishing food. Can we eat a few bites? I'll help you." Rounding his bed, she plunked down the tray on a small table.

Jack moaned, "God no, nothing. I hurt too much. I feel like I been stomped on by a wild stallion—maybe a whole herd of 'em. Can't Doc stop this pain?"

"You had painkiller last night. He says you are to get along without it if you can."

"Well, I can't. Get some. Pronto!" Jack wondered what was wrong with this woman? Didn't she understand plain lingo? He glared at this buzzing horsefly.

"Doctor Handy will be in soon. You can ask him. Meanwhile, let's try to eat this porridge. And here is some lovely applesauce." The nurse circled his bed, fussing with his covers.

Damn woman, he thought, she glides around like a toy horse on wheels. "I don't want anything to eat, Sister. Why don't you get the hell out of here and leave me alone? Just tell Doc to get in here."

His language shocked the men who occupied beds on either side of him, but the woman seemed unconcerned. She paused at the door of the ward, a gentle smile still on her face.

"Hey, where's that Velarde woman? She go home?" Jack called out.

"No, she's much too ill for that."

"Ill? That hellcat's as healthy as a horse. Brought me in here, didn't she?"

"Oh, you mean Miss Velarde. I thought you meant her mother. She's here too."

"I mean that vixen that pumped lead into me. Where is she?" In his anger Jack forgot and propped himself up on his right elbow. He collapsed, groaning in pain. "Damn, she really winged me."

"Here's Dr. Handy now. Speak with him about your needs."

The doctor made his way from bed to bed, checking on his patients. When he reached Jack, he pulled aside the dressing on his shoulder. "It's a clean wound. The bullet went clear through. You'll have to give it a few weeks to heal, but it will be fine."

"What about my gut?"

Dr. Handy lifted the dressing on his patient's abdomen. "Just a scratch. Bullet grazed you. Probably ricocheted off something."

Jack peered down at his belly, realizing that this wound didn't pain him nearly as much as his shoulder did. "Yep, you're right. Expect I've had cat scratches worse than that. But that damn loco female was out to kill me. A wonder she didn't."

"Miss Velarde told me about the shooting. Plans to turn herself in. She's here with her mother right now. She did you a service bringing you here in that flood. Don't forget that."

Jack harrumphed. But he was glad that Teresa was still here. He'd make that woman pay for taking shots at him like he was a jackrabbit. "How about some pain killer, Doc?"

"You don't need any. Morphine's powerful stuff. Pain will go away in no time." Handy frowned and gazed out the window.

Jack had heard the stories in town about the doctor's wife being hooked on the stuff, about the divorce, and Handy's threats to kill Frank Heney, the lawyer who had taken up her case. Heney was handling Ned Harrington's will, and Jack considered him a fair-minded man. But in a showdown the lawyer would be no match for the doctor. Handy was a rough customer, all right. Jack once saw him in a fight; madder than a bull, he had trounced the other fellow.

The doctor said, "You're free to leave the hospital tomorrow, but take it easy for a few days. Come to my office Saturday."

Jack fumed. He couldn't take any more time off from his job. He was damn well going to leave the hospital today, but not until he had seen that madwoman who had put holes in him. He was willing to bet his last six bits that Teresa would never pull a gun on him again. When a nurse came in later to change his dressing, he demanded his clothes. He dressed and set out to locate her.

Slumped in a wicker chair beside her mother's bed, Teresa awakened in confusion before she remembered last night. She had left Jack at the hospital and stabled Pegasus and the carthorse at the Velarde corral where she also left the wagon. Then she had walked to the casita. After four hours of sleep she had saddled Pegasus and returned to the hospital. Though she wanted to check on Jack, she decided to see her mother first. She dragged in a chair from a nearby alcove, planning to sit by her mother for a few minutes but had fallen asleep.

Now rays of sun slanted through the window. She watched her mother's ashen face, willing her to open her eyes. Her chest heaved as her body battled for breath, her short guttural gasps of breath growing louder until there was a pause. Teresa waited in alarm for her mother to start breathing again.

Earlier, she had concocted a story of finding Jack on the road south of Tucson, but when she saw Dr. Handy in the corridor, she had blurted out the truth. She knew she'd be tried in a court of law for attempted murder and face prison or perhaps something worse. Lord God, she thought to herself, what happened to my anger? Could the mere sight of his suffering cause it to dissolve? Do I love that worthless creature?

She sat up in astonishment at the sight of Jack in the doorway, red-faced, his right arm in a sling.

"You murdering bitch!" he roared, stomping into the ward, his eyes glittering with fire. "I'm going to see you put in jail for what you done to me. Good thing you aren't a crack shot. Damn you! Look at me. Shoulder busted up. I'm madder'n hell at you. But I'm gonna fix your wagon in court. You can bet your boots on that."

Patients on the ward turned to look at Jack. Now it's started, Teresa thought. Conflicting emotions dragged her first in one direction, then in another; she felt like a frightened cottontail rabbit running to and fro in lantern light.

"Damn! You get a cockeyed notion in your head and shoot people very often?" Approaching the bed, he went on in a more moderate tone, "Good thing you didn't hit anything vital."

"But your other wound—"

"Just a cat scratch."

"I'm glad to see you're on your feet." Teresa sighed. Why did she want to comfort him when she despised him? For God's sake, he was unspeakably vile. She folded her arms tightly over her stomach, suddenly realizing she felt sick and could scarcely control the urge to vomit. Why must she endure these relentless pendulum swings in her nature? Why couldn't she choose a course of action and be steadfast in it?

She turned to look at her mother, willing herself to think about her, not this wretch who spewed anger as if it were molten lava. Teresa squared her shoulders and faced Jack, speaking softly. "I'll tell you again why I wanted to kill you, Jack O'Brien. Or should I call you Spike O'Brien?"

"Spike? No one's called me that since I was a greenhorn. Where'd you get that handle?"

"Do you know the woman in this bed?"

"No. Never seen her before."

"Take a closer look." Teresa rose from her chair and gently turned her mother's face so Jack could see the scar. "I'll help you. She's my mother. Her first name is Jessie. Her maiden name was Copeland."

Jack was silent for a moment. "Lord! Jessie Copeland? She's *your* mother? Damn, this is hard to believe. Uh, I'm sorry she's so bad off. What's her ailment?"

"Hush," Teresa whispered. She ushered Jack to an alcove where two chairs and a bench faced the windmill. Its wheels were barely turning. Teresa glanced back at her mother to see if she was still breathing.

They sat down on the bench, and she told him of her mother's near drowning in the flood. "So you see, Jessie's my mother. I learned about that cattle raid you and three others were on near Tubaca. I learned that you are my father. Just as I told you out there before I shot you."

"By God, no!" Jack shook his head, a look of consternation on his face. "You got it all wrong, Teresa, I swear it's the truth. It was my partner, Ned Harrington who done it. I come across them just after he'd—just after it happened to her."

Teresa was startled; she recalled the name Harrington from Multaney's story. He was one of the four cattle rustlers involved in the hoax. "Where does he live? I'll ask him about your story."

"God almighty, Teresa, you can't shoot *him*. Ned's dead. He was my partner off and on for over thirty years. In Mexico a lot of that time."

"This Ned is the one who attacked my mother? How can I believe what you say? You haven't been truthful up to this point. Telling me you were looking for a niece." Teresa shook her head.

"Ned didn't trust me to deliver his money to the woman he wronged or to the daughter, but before he died he asked me to find either one of them—found you both, it looks like. There's a will in Frank Heney's office here in Tucson. Ned's will. It's got your mother's name in it, and it tells the whole story."

"Will? What are you talking about?"

"I'm telling you that your mother is about to inherit some money."

Teresa glanced at him in amazement. "Tell me your story from the beginning."

"Well, about what he did to her down in Tubaca—I swear, the older Ned got, the more he fretted over it. 'Perdonar la deuda'—it's all he could say on his deathbed. Cancel the debt. Always cancel the debt. He was like some critter with a festering thorn in its side. What he done was terrible and he knew it."

"I don't understand. What happened?"

"You see, back in fifty-four, me, Ned, and the other two was working for a contractor. Supplied beef to a couple of merchants in Tucson. These fellows wasn't too perticular how we come by the beef. And some of us hit upon this plan to get all painted up as Apaches. We rode out and cut us out a few head of cattle at one of the spreads down there. We could get away with it, because them damned Apaches was cleaning out a lot of little ranches—they was pretty bad back then. People were sore about that."

"What has all this to do with my mother?" Teresa asked.

"Ned had met up with her some place or other in Tubaca. She

was a real pretty gal—your mother. Well, the long and the short of it was that Ned fell for her in a big way. He was good looking, a mestizo, wasn't real dark or anything, but she wouldn't so much as spit on him."

"She has never been kind to Mexicans. Strangely enough, she married one. My father. . . I mean Hector Velarde."

Jack turned to glance at Jessie. "You know, I thought I'd already met your mother in the store one day. Some nice old lady said her name was Velarde. Said she was your mother."

"I don't know about that. Oh, I suppose it could have been my aunt, but I don't know why she would say that."

17 "A Little Accident" ❖ July 27

"Fue una broma, y nada mass." Socorro had quietly entered the ward and was standing beside the bench. "Anyway, it seemed a harmless joke at the time."

"Tía Socorro, I didn't know you were here," Teresa said.

"Lito brought me."

"Sit down, Tía. Mr. O'Brien, meet my aunt, Señorita Velarde. This is Jack O'Brien. Oh, I forgot, you've already met. He's telling a story you'll want to hear."

"¿Señorita? Oh, I see I had it wrong that day when I thought you were Señora Velarde, Teresa's mother. Sorry." Jack looked abashed. "¿Prefiere que hablemos español, Señorita Velarde?"

"No, Mr. O'Brien. I understand your tongue quite well," Socorro answered.

Teresa retold the beginning of Jack's story and asked him to continue.

"Anyway, just after dusk we was sneaking around in the corral like Apaches when I saw Ned wasn't with us," Jack said. "Then I heard this screaming in the barn and I knew damn well what he was up to. Knew it was Jessie Copeland. I ran in there to stop him, but it was all over. She was screaming like a stuck pig—damn, excuse me, I mean she was yelling something awful, calling out his name."

"How did she recognize this man if he was dressed as an Indian?" Socorro asked.

"Well, ma'am, he was pretty close up to her and she knew his face." Socorro said, "Go on."

"She was screaming and they was struggling and the lantern got knocked over. Kerosene. Started a fire. I stomped it out where it was spreading in the hay. Her clothes was on fire, and Ned covered her with his shirt to get it out."

Teresa moaned. "Oh my poor, poor mother. Why was she in the barn?"

"I don't know," Jack said. "We'd sent Ned to close the barn door."

"What happened after that, Mr. O'Brien?" Socorro's face showed no sympathy for Jack, only shock and distaste.

"Not much more to tell. One night a month or so later he snuck back to the ranch to try to make up with her. Slipped through her bedroom window and told her he was real sorry for what he did, that he loved her and all that. But all she did was scream bloody murder. He jumped out of the window and lit out fast."

"There was a trial," Teresa reminded him. "Weren't you accused of rustling?"

"Yes, but it wasn't much of a trial. You know how things was then, not much law around. A bunch of citizens got together. Most of them was friends of this rancher we worked for. They believed us when we told them we was just having a little fun. We got off with a warning from the judge. Boys will be boys, was the way he put it. He had pull, I'll give him that. The whole story never came out. The judge told us to vamoose for a while. White and Archibald drifted on over to Texas. Ned and I went back down to Sonora."

"Then how did you know Jessie had a girl—had me?" Teresa asked.

"We worked at a ranch just over the border, and Ned went back a few times to see if Jessie might change her mind about him. He was that far gone on her. But the last time he went he found out she'd had a baby girl and got married and gone off to Tucson."

"I wonder why she married my father—I mean, married Hector Velarde," Teresa amended.

"Ned said those religious people she lived with made her get hitched. Truth was they didn't want her around anymore after what happened to their barn. Burned down. But in all those years Ned never forgot he had a daughter. Sometimes when we was sitting at our campfire, he'd talk about Jessie and his daughter. He was right sorry about the whole thing. I don't think he ever stopped loving Jessie. Never got hitched up to anyone."

Teresa's head spun. If Jessie had married Eduardo, how would her life have turned out? Would she have lived in Sonora?

Jack was explaining to Socorro how Teresa had become an heiress.

"This Señor Harrington acquired his fortune in Mexico?" Socorro asked.

Jack grinned. "Sure did. He was one shrewd hombre when it came to money."

Then Socorro asked a question that Teresa had wanted to ask. "How much is this fortune?"

"Don't rightly know," Jack admitted. "It's in that will and I believe it's good-sized. He had money stashed away and a ranch near Magdalena."

Socorro asked, "What is your interest in all this?"

"Ned's will includes a fee for me—I guess they call it a legacy—if I found Jessie Copeland or her daughter. Now I'm in the chips. I got fifteen hundred dollars coming to me." Jack smiled at Teresa.

Teresa stared out the window. The windmill's arms had stopped. She hurried to her mother's bedside to check on her. Jessie still breathed. The morning sun struck her face, turning the red scar as bright as the tulips in the appliquéd coverlet on her bed—Jessie's own handiwork that Manuela brought in the night before. "It will brighten the room for Gammy," the girl had explained.

Teresa pulled the muslin curtains across the window and turned her mother's burned cheek away from the sun before returning to the others. The three sat in silence for a few moments, and then Teresa said, "It must have been a terrible time for my mother. So young. But I still don't know why she would turn down one Mexican and then marry another." A puzzled frown creased her forehead.

"As Mr. O'Brien said, she must have been forced into marriage by those people she was living with. She never spoke to me about how she met my brother," Socorro said. "But I think by the time Hector came courting she was in such low spirits she didn't care what happened to her. When she came to Tucson, she was always sad. I was the only one who could lighten her heart. She loved me, but only tolerated Hector. Now that I know the whole terrible story, I doubt that she could truly love any man, no matter what his race was."

Socorro turned to Jack. "Señor O'Brien, how's your shoulder? Luis told me of your mishap."

Teresa knew her aunt had heard the whole story. All Tucson would soon know. Teresa met Jack's eyes that shone with a shrewd animal gleam. "Let's say I met with a little accident," he said.

"It was no accident. I meant to kill him. As you can see, my aim was none too accurate," Teresa said. "You will doubtless press charges, Mr. O'Brien."

Socorro looked at Teresa, her eyes wide with surprise. "¿Matarlo? Por Dios, que dices! Supe que fue un accidente."

Jack stared at Teresa and said smoothly, "No, Miss Velarde, you were acting as you saw fit. Sure am glad you just hit my shoulder. And I'm sure glad you got me here to get patched up. Took pity on me, I guess."

Their gaze still locked on each other, Teresa fancied she saw the glow of love in Jack's face. But she was confounded by his shift from fury to benign acceptance of her murderous attempt. Teresa breathed a sigh. Of course, greed had defused his anger and brought on this sudden charm; he viewed an heiress in a different light.

"Will someone please tell me what this is about? Teresa, en el nombre de Dios, why did you want to kill him?" Socorro demanded.

"Because he had come courting me as a suitor, but then I believed he was also my father."

"Your father! You thought Mr. O'Brien had—had been with Jessie?" Pain distorted Socorro's face. "No wonder you wanted to kill him. Oh Teresita, why didn't you come to me?"

"Because you would have stopped me." Teresa's voice was scarcely louder than a whisper. "I had already disgraced the family name by being with Jack without a chaperon. I simply couldn't tell you what I learned at the newspaper about the raid and what I suspected about my poor mother."

"Oh, Palomita," Socorro said sadly. "Yo lo habría entendido. I would have understood."

Teresa sobbed. "Oh, Tía Socorro, I've disappointed everyone. You and Jessie—mostly Jessie. If only she would recover so I could tell her how sorry I am. Oh, how she has suffered."

"Ven, Palomita. Mi hijita." Socorro opened her arms, kissed her niece, and stroked her hair. Jack watched the two women, his head bowed.

Through her tears, Teresa glanced out the window. The windmill cranked on.

18 Manuela ❖ July 29 and 30

Members of the Velarde family spent the day at St. Mary's, but as the hours stretched out and Jessie's condition remained the same, they went home at dusk. Luis and Teresa stayed on. One of the Sisters who came to check Jessie said she would live only a few hours more.

After she left Teresa said, "I've heard that nurses often know when death is approaching before the doctors do."

"They are probably more familiar with the patient's body from hour to hour than doctors are," Luis said. "Teresa, I've arranged for a Catholic funeral mass."

"Jessie's not Catholic."

Luis shook his head. "Perhaps not a practicing Catholic, but she was married in the Church. It's for the family, Teresa."

She shrugged her shoulders and made no further objections to his plans. After all, Jessie should be buried with her husband. Remembering the perspective lesson at St. Joseph's, she thought, at last their paths would converge at the end of the road.

At midnight Luis went home, encouraging Teresa to do the same—that she needed a good night's sleep. Teresa replied that she would stay with her mother.

She held Jessie's hand, gazing out the hospital window, listening to the windmill. Across the dark river and fields, the muddy town was asleep, a pinpoint of light flickering here and there. Jessie's harsh breathing punctuated Teresa's quiet, murmured prayers and added to the polyphony of sound in the ward—patients snoring and springs squeaking as they turned over in bed.

Jessie's hand was cold, her breathing sometimes stopped for a few moments, and Teresa's own heartbeat quickened as she leaned forward to study her mother's face in the lamp light. Jessie's chest heaved, a breath was caught, another grain of sand in the glass dropped down. Teresa squeezed the cold fingers that sometimes twitched, though no longer in response to hers. Her mother's leave taking was nearly over, but the final retreat was slow. Why was death so unhurried? Teresa's initial guilt at this thought gave way to reasoned patience. Her mother would die in her own good time, but it tore at Teresa to see this being that once was Jessie maintain its futile attempt to hold onto life when the mind was gone.

The night sky slid imperceptibly from its inky resolve to rule in darkness. Stars paled. The gray light of dawn was surrendering to streaks of vermillion when Jessie Velarde's struggle for breath ended. "Descansa, mamá. Rest now."

The air was still, the windmill silent. Her eyes on the Santa Catalina Mountains, Teresa deliberately suspended thought and focused on the distinctive peaks as the sun lit them up with rosy hues. When she was a little girl, she had made out shapes in the distant peaks: a pipe organ, a finger pointing to heaven, the back of a reclining cat or the face of an Indian. Lito told her that Spaniards called the peaks La Iglesia, and she could see the church. She knelt and prayed for her mother's soul. For the past few days Teresa's outward grief had spilled in quiet tears that ebbed and flowed like a tide. The tears of moments ago were dry on her cheeks. None fell now. Time had not yet healed the pain inside her—the pain inspired by her mother's sad, wasted life. She wondered if it ever would.

She wearily rose and went to summon a Sister.

Two hours later Luis and Socorro came into the ward. They knelt by the bed and prayed. A short time later, Dr. Handy came in to sign the death certificate. Before departing Luis paid the hospital bill and thanked the staff for their solicitous care of Jessie.

At the Velarde home the women spent the day gathering supplies and cooking for the velorio to be held that evening. In the kitchen Socorro said to Teresa, "Luis arranged to have the undertaker bring her body here this afternoon. Do you want to choose a dress for your mother for el velorio? In this heat we can't delay the—" She broke off with a sob.

Teresa embraced her aunt. "Yes. She has two good dresses which she seldom wore."

"How I wish Margarita could be here for the funeral, but it isn't likely." Socorro sighed.

"We sent my sister a letter last week. She may make it in time."

August 26, 1876 ~ Tía Socorro came up to Tucson to help Olivia with her new baby. Luis wanted to name her Manuela Socorro, but Olivia insisted on naming her after her mother too. Manuela María Socorro. Quite a mouthful for the little one.

At the casa grande Luis shook his daughter awake. "Manuelita, your grandmother is now in heaven." He held her while she sobbed, and when she grew calm he said, "This evening the priest from San Agustín's will come for the velorio. You must help your mother today."

Despite having seen her grandmother's gray face and listened to her labored breathing in the hospital, Manuela still couldn't believe that her Gammy was gone—the one who had told her stories and made clothes for her dolls. As a young child she had visited her other grandmother, Abuela Velarde, in Tubutama, Sonora. The early morning routine of this grandmother had deeply impressed her. Her abuela always sat at a window after completing her toilet—a cleansing she considered almost holy—whispering her oraciones. Manuela had vowed to emulate her, and from that day she had kept her vow. After she washed and dressed, she knelt at the window for her daily devotions.

Manuela smelled the aroma of tortillas and hurried to the kitchen. Tía Socorro, her mother, and two next door neighbors had been working over a hot comal since daybreak, making thirty dozen tortillas. Tía Teresa was chopping pork into cubes for posole.

After breakfast Manuela helped her mother move the parlor furniture to make space for the casket and additional chairs. Olivia frowned. "I'm afraid it will be much too crowded, but it's the only room large enough. I'll dust in here, Manuela. You bring in the chairs from the dining room and then help Teresa carry hers over."

The year before, her mother had ordered a new parlor suite from a catalog—two petit point chairs, rocker, armchair, and plush sofa. Manuela noticed that her mother's face glowed with pride, much like the dark veneered sofa table top she was polishing.

After Manuela helped arrange the room, her mother posted her at the parlor window to watch for the undertaker. Though grieving about Gammy's death, Manuela was delighted to sit quietly with needlework that was meant for her hope chest. She had already hemmed lengths of fine linen for hand towels and could now embroider them. She adjusted the metal hoop around the poppy design Tía Teresa had drawn on the linen, and with her needle pulled orange floss through it. She felt a tinge of guilt about enjoying pleasure at this solemn time, so she put on her serious face. Never having been part of a velorio before and nervous about what the day would bring, she reminded herself that Gammy was now at peace. Then tears streaked down her cheeks.

The undertaker's carriage drawn by two black horses pulled up outside, and Manuela hastily wiped her face on her sleeve. In the sunlight ornate gold letters gleamed on the black carriage, "E. J. Smith, Undertaker." Through the oval window of the carriage Manuela saw the coffin and felt a prickle of fear. Breathless, she ran to tell her mother the undertaker had arrived.

In the parlor Manuela watched as her Tía Abuela Socorro washed her grandmother's body, placed pennies on the eyelids, stuffed cotton up her nostrils to prevent the escape of unpleasant odors, and bound her jaw with a silk handkerchief. Dismayed at her Gammy's appearance, Manuela protested. Her great aunt assured all this would be removed before the velorio. Though it was difficult to manipulate the stiff body, Teresa dressed her mother in a gown of ivory silk with a high lace collar. Manuela was fascinated as the two women applied rouge and powder. She thought her grandmother's face looked peaceful.

Then Tía Teresa insisted that the coffin be reversed on the trestles supporting it. She said her mother's scar must not be noticed by approaching mourners. So used to her grandmother's face, Manuela was surprised by her aunt's concern. The scar was her Gammy's special mark, she said. Then Tía Teresa had told her that her grandmother had been burned by fire, and it would have been her wish to present the good side of her face.

Manuela wanted to question her aunt about the fire, but at that moment Stella and Hector ran into the room full of excitement, announcing that Tía Margarita and their cousins had arrived. The whole family rushed to the street.

Lito handed Margarita down from the wagon, his wide face beaming. "I found her at the stage coach office." Lito's face grew serious. "I'm sorry about your mother. Lo siento mucho con saber que Señora Velarde falleció."

Teresa wrapped her arms around the short Yaqui. "Gracias, mí amigo."

With nieces and nephews dancing around her, Margarita was barely able to move to the front door. Socorro cajoled the children inside with a promise of chocolate. Teresa and Manuela each took one of Margarita's hands and led her into the parlor. They stood stiffly beside Jessie's coffin for a moment, then turned to embrace each other, breaking into tears. Margarita leaned down and kissed her mother's cheek. "Que fria esta, como mármol," she cried.

"Ah, Margarita, Jessie would take that as a tribute that she is like marble, like a Greek statue."

Manuela thought that her grandmother did indeed look like a lovely but cold statue.

That evening the family greeted men clad in dark clothes, women in black dresses and rebozos as they arrived at the casa grande. Mourners brought food, the universal balm at the time of mourning, and Teresa and Manuela deposited the platters and bowls in the kitchen or in the dining room. Pots of posole simmered on the kitchen stove, and stacks of tortillas waited in the warming oven.

Guests filed into the candlelit parlor, clutching their rosaries and kneeling at the wooden coffin. At half past six the priest from San Agustín arrived to conduct the service. The chairs in the room were soon filled, so many stood while they said the rosary. Often those who came to mourn at a velorio would stay up all night to pray and tell pleasant or humorous stories about the deceased. But Jessie Velarde had never made the effort to fit into the Mexican community, and few people had tales to share. During the evening mourners refreshed themselves in the dining room with posole, tortillas, melons, cheeses, and pastries. Before midnight they had said their farewells.

Growing faint in the hot, close room, Teresa slipped away to the casita. Wandering from room to room, she touched photographs on the piano, her mother's sewing basket by her chair, her large cup on a kitchen shelf for her morning coffee. When she sat down in the parlor, she immediately jumped up to strip the linen from her mother's bed and take down the curtain around it. She folded and stacked the dusty curtain and bedclothes at the foot of the bed. Unable to bear the sight of the naked mattress, she was sorry she had removed the curtains. She slumped into a chair at the kitchen table, her head on her arms.

Teresa awoke with a stiff neck. Her anxiety about Jack beset her anew. She was still stunned that she would inherit a large sum of money. If Jack courted her now, it was for her wealth. Clearly, he was nothing more than a calculating prospector drawn by the color of gold—*her* gold.

But what of her needs? For years she had yearned for a husband. Should she accept him, knowing him for what he was? Marry him despite his motives? Certainly he would ask her to be his wife. At the hospital before he left, he squeezed her hand. A thought flitted through her mind before she returned to the velorio: Why didn't Jack respond to her letters or even so much as mention them?

19 The Funeral ❖ July 31

The next day Teresa arose before dawn to help prepare food for a gathering after the funeral. Chased out of the kitchen, Luis ate breakfast in the dining room. Teresa went in to pour him a second cup of coffee. "Luis, are you enjoying being home on a weekday? Not having to charm customers at the Emporium?"

Luis blew on the steaming coffee. "Yes, but it does seem strange. Everything that has happened these past few days has been strange. Your—well, I can't imagine you trying to murder a man, nor becoming an heiress."

Teresa was relieved that his tone wasn't accusatory. His reaction would have been so different if she'd killed Jack. "I can scarcely believe all these things myself. Luis, if he had violated Jessie, wouldn't you have wanted to kill him?"

"Probably, but I wouldn't have missed." He smiled up at Teresa.

In the kitchen the Velarde women made tamales. The master of the operation, Socorro mixed the masa (corn meal) with lard, spices, and broth from the beef she had cooked the day before. She added salt to the mixture in the form of a cross. "Para bendecir la masa, to bless the dough," she explained.

In the palm of one hand the women overlapped two cornhusks that had been soaked in water to soften them and ladled masa into them. This was followed by a dollop of beef chunks mixed with chiles and spices that Socorro had cooked the day before. Next, they folded the husks over this mixture to make a package. Dozens of tamales in large covered pans would steam for two hours in the ovens in both Verlarde houses.

Supervising the cooking, Olivia bustled between kitchen and patio. On the fire pit outside where water was heated on washday, two neighbors were stirring a huge kettle of menudo. Luis lounged with the other men in the shade of the ramada, smoking, and now and then sneaking a drink of whiskey from their flasks. Luis chopped mesquite wood for the cooking fires. The cousins romped in the patio or the house until the women found them underfoot and shooed them out again.

In her long apron Manuela carried dishes and cutlery to the dining table. She told Teresa that Señor O'Brien was at the door. "I put him in the dining room, porque Gammy está en la sala."

"Gracias, Manuela. Tell him I'll be there directly." Teresa took off her apron and sighed in resignation. Nothing had changed, nothing could happen. Jack, his arm still in a sling, stood as she entered.

"Good day, Mr. O'Brien. How is your shoulder?" She gripped the back of a dining chair.

"It's mending, Señorita Velarde. I'm awful sorry about your mother." He nodded his head toward the parlor. "I heard the funeral's this afternoon. I'd like to go. That all right with you?"

"If you wish." Teresa noticed that he spoke soberly, displaying none of his glib charm. She sat in one of the chairs. "Please be seated."

"I guess she didn't have an easy life. Heard tell she didn't get out and about much."

"No, she was a recluse."

Noting the puzzled look on Jack's face, Teresa said, "I mean she kept to herself. She wasn't especially happy—oh, there were times when she was happy—in her way." Teresa recalled the moments when Jessie's eyes would light up when she read a story to her or listened to music at a concert. There had been occasional moments of lightness and joy that stood out in the drab patchwork of Jessie's life.

"I come to tell you what I've been doing about this legacy of yours. Met with Frank Heney yesterday—the lawyer. You'll need to come in and bring your birth certificate and a witness to speak for you. We can set it up for tomorrow, if that's a good time for you."

"That'll be fine."

"After that I got to get back to the ranch before I'm laid off. Sent word about this little accident, but that'll cut no mustard with the boss. He already gave me all the sissy chores because of that bout of grippe. Truth is, I don't know if I even have a job anymore."

"I hope you do. . . Mr. O'Brien, why didn't you answer my letters? You did get them, didn't you?"

"Yes. Wes told me what was in the letters." Jack looked down at his boots, twisting his mustache between thumb and forefinger. "I'm not much of one to write."

Teresa instantly realized why he didn't answer her letters. This man, who spoke such beautiful Spanish and who generally seemed so sure of himself in most ways, couldn't read. In spite of the pity she felt, she relentlessly continued, "You didn't answer because you don't know how to read—or write?"

"Book learning is nothing I can brag about. Didn't stay in school much. Then I ran away from home when I was fourteen."

Teresa was ashamed she had sought to humble him. She said softly, "I see. I'm sorry."

Jack patted his mustache, laughed and tossed his head. "Don't you worry, I've learned how to take care of Jack O'Brien. Learned in the school of hard knocks."

"I see. What time at Mr. Heney's, Jack?"

"Tomorrow at one o'clock in the afternoon. I'll come by here to take you." He leaned forward and brushed her cheek with a kiss before he picked up his hat on the entry table and swaggered out the door.

Teresa was both thrilled and annoyed at his temerity.

The last brash clang from the bell in the tall pointed spire of San Agustín reverberated and faded. Teresa stood before the arched entry of the stone facade, Mercedes beside her, a knot of Luis's children gathered around them. Teresa searched the plaza for a sign of Jack, but didn't see him.

Olivia officiously arranged the children in the order she deemed appropriate, took Teresa's arm and led her flock away, leaving Mercedes standing alone. Teresa knew that Olivia had always looked down on Mercedes because she was a mere seamstress.

Smiling brightly and apparently taking no notice of the rebuff, Mercedes smoothed the fingers of her black gloves.

May 21, 1889 ~ Today Mercedes & I & Lito picnicked in Sabino Canyon. The desert is so lovely in spring—the bright yellow flowers of the palo verdes where bees were buzzing & the red of the ocotillo. Lito said that deer know how to stand still & look like ocotillo, their horns like the spiny branches. Then he sang a song about deer & how his people tie red ribbons on the horns in the deer dance to represent the blossoms. It was a wonderful day. Lito and Mercedes are my very best friends. And Socorro.

As they walked down the center aisle, Teresa noticed that not many people were in the dark church. A few tradesmen and their wives had come out of respect for Luis. During the homily the priest mentioned the flood as the primary cause of Jessie's death. Teresa's mind wandered. Of the elements Jessie feared—air, fire, earth and water—the Kansas cyclone was the air that had ended her childhood, and when she was a young woman a terrible fire had scarred her, and the desert earth had shriveled her soul. But in the end, water had overcome her; she had drowned in the water in her lungs. Now earth had claimed her body and heaven her soul.

In the dusty plaza two rented carriages awaited the family behind a black hearse. A half-dozen one-horse buggies were forming a procession behind the vehicles. Waiting horses stamped their feet and swished their tails to combat swarms of flies. Teresa lifted her skirts to navigate through mounds of horse dung to reach one of the carriages. The smell of manure warmed by intense heat rose to her nostrils, and she drew in shallow breaths. She lifted her hand to her black-veiled hat, half intending to lift it off and fan her face. Propriety prevailing, she left it in place. Rivulets of sweat poured down her back.

Teresa spied Jack climbing onto his buckboard in front of Dr. Handy's office. Her teeth clamped together, Teresa scolded herself for watching for Jack from the moment she had come to the plaza. Why was she still interested in this unsuitable man? She should put him out of her mind.

The procession headed north on Court Street. Memories flocked to Teresa as they crossed Alameda. Once named Cemetery Street, it was the site of the old National Cemetery at Stone Avenue and had once contained the Velarde family plot. A few years after Hector

Velarde's death, Tucson's officials appropriated the cemetery for the new railroad, and Tucsonans were forced to move the remains of their loved ones. Luis arranged for the disinterment and reburial of the Velarde family in the new cemetery.

The shattering grief she had felt when her father died was different from this mixture of pity and regret her mother's death inspired. The two losses melded into a deeper sorrow, flowing into the emptiness surrounding her like a torrent of rainwater in an arroyo. But Teresa sadly reminded herself that Hector, who had taken her on horseback rides and told her stories of his army days, the Papá she adored, must now be considered a stepfather. Yet, in her memories of their times together he was always her father.

January 16, 1869 ~ Tonight we sang songs around the piano. Afterward Papá told a story about fighting Apaches in his army days. He said they rode over very rough country for 5 nights to attack an Apache ranchería in Arivaipa Canyon. They surprised Apaches & killed many & took some as prisoners. He showed me a scar on his leg. I asked if it was from an arrow. He laughed and said no, a horse had kicked him. They had killed many Indians on that raid but Capt. Tidball was happiest about getting the stock back.

The procession halted at the cemetery. The Velarde plot, surrounded by a freshly painted white picket fence, was carefully tended and adorned with flowers—Olivia's handiwork. Whenever Luis could spare the money over the years, he had replaced wooden markers with stone. Perhaps Jessie would have scoffed at the mass and burial, but Teresa was persuaded that it was appropriate for Jessie to rest next to Hector in this peaceful setting. Again she visualized two lines representing their lives at last converging on the horizon, obedient to the rules of perspective.

Dark clouds mercifully masked the fierce late afternoon sun as the family gathered around the flower-bedecked coffin beside the gaping hole where it would be lowered. As Teresa stood gazing down, she became dizzy, an experience totally foreign to her. She turned to Mercedes who stood behind her and whispered, "No me siento bien. I must sit down."

Mercedes took Teresa's elbow and guided her to the Verlarde carriage. "¿Qué tienes, Teresa?" she asked with a frown.

"It's all been too much for me."

"It's understandable. Your mother, the heat. . . but isn't this also about Jack?"

"Oh, Mercedes, can you believe I should be so upset about a cowhand? I don't even know my own mind anymore." Teresa sobbed, hoarse cries emanating from the depth of her being.

"Estimada amiga, I must tell you something. I don't want to hide anything from my good friend. I was the first woman Jack talked to when he came looking for that niece of his."

"Oh, no!" Tears flowed anew. "Mercedes, you never said a word to me about it!"

"How could I tell you that day you came to me all aglow with happiness? Not on your life. Besides, I saw him before he courted you. But there is something important you must know. Jack truly cares for you."

"How do you know that?" Teresa looked at her in disbelief.

"He told me as we walked out of the church today. You are the first woman he has truly admired—even though you took a potshot at him. Maybe because you had the nerve to. Creo que sinceramente, te ama."

"Loves me! Mentiras! He loves my money. Did he tell you about that?"

"Yes, he did. I am so happy for you, mí amiga. That's not the reason he wants you—at least not all of it. He asked me to persuade you to marry him. Teresita, give him a chance. Perhaps he's the great love you seek." Mercedes took her hand.

Teresa peered at the departing crowd. Jack was turning his wagon about and pulling away. She leaned back and closed her eyes. Was what she felt for Jack truly love or merely passing infatuation? "I don't know for sure. Perhaps he is."

"In your heart I think you know." She pressed her friend's hand. "Look, it's beginning to rain."

The following morning Socorro and Teresa sat in the ramada sipping glasses of lemonade, Teresa with a book open on her lap, her aunt sewing patches on pants for Olivia's boys.

"Por favor, Teresita, would you thread my needle? My old eyes aren't sharp enough."

Teresa sighed as she complied with her aunt's request. "Pensaba en Jessie."

"Me lo pense. I thought so." Socorro took back the needle. "Gracias, Palomita."

"I miss her." Tears welled up in Teresa's eyes.

"You're bound to. You lived with her all your life. You were a good daughter, and she mothered you as best she could." Socorro leaned over to pat her niece's hand.

"I know that now." Teresa closed her book and dabbed her eyes with her handkerchief. "Jack's gone to Mexico to complete the sale of Ned's ranch. I hope it doesn't take too long."

"Estas cosas toman tiempo, Palomita, particularmente en Mexico."

"I worry about this sale. What if Jack makes a deal on the side and pockets the money?"

"I don't believe he could do that. You told me that Frank Heney had an evaluation of the properties that were to be sold. And, remember, there will be a contract that Jack must bring back to you. . . Teresa, if you are considering marrying this man you must trust him."

"What makes you think I'm considering marrying him? His past record gives me little reason to."

"You have been thinking of it for weeks."

"Perhaps I have, but I seem to go back and forth. First, it is yes, and then no. Maybe you are right. Today it seems to be yes." But first, she thought, I must find the way to reform him, to mold him to my satisfaction.

Socorro bit off the thread and folded little Hector's breeches and laid them aside. "You must work to earn the understanding that never existed between Hector and Jessie. It's building love, adobe by adobe, on a common ground of trust. From what I have seen of life, married love doesn't spring up by itself.

"Let me tell you a story, Palomita. It really happened. Not far from Tubutama there are two small villages, a few miles apart. Two girls, one from each village, found work as maids in a great hacienda near Tubutama. Stella, a pretty girl, had a boyfriend, but Esperanza was as ugly as an old mesquite stump. Everyone said she was destined to be una solterona.

"Pretty Stella was engaged to be married to Pedro, a boy in her village, but she kept putting off the wedding for one reason or another—usually a trifling reason—sometimes she said Pedro was trifling with other girls in the village."

"Was he?"

Socorro shrugged. "I don't know about that. Could be. Anyway, a date was finally set and Stella left her job at the hacienda to go home and prepare for the big day. Esperanza got permission from the hacendado to attend the wedding. All the wedding guests were assembled in the chapel. They waited and waited. Finally they learned from Stella's father that she had once more changed her mind about marrying Pedro. The priest who had come from Tubutama to conduct the wedding mass was very angry. The groom waiting at the altar was forlorn. Poor Pedro just stood there, his head bowed in shame, crying big tears. Esperanza was so sad for him that she marched up to the altar and took his hand and said, 'Pedro, if you'll have me, I'll marry you.' Mind you, she had never met him before."

"And were they married?"

"As quickly as a cat can catch a mouse. They still are, and I'm told have many children running around that little village."

"Oh, Socorro, that's a wonderful tale. I suppose it is true."

"Sí, es verdad." Socorro chuckled. "But the padre who married them told me the story, and, knowing him, he may have touched it up a little."

"I suppose there is a message for me. Seize my opportunity before it slips away?"

"If the shoe fits—" Socorro laughed again.

Teresa smiled and took Socorro's hand. "You are a wise woman, Tía Socorro, especially for one who never married."

"All the better to observe the matrimonial state more clearly."

Teresa sighed. "How I wish Jack would return with his mission accomplished."

"Palomita, don't worry about him. He'll be back. He won't miss the Fiesta."

They sat quietly for a few minutes. The strained relationship that had existed over the summer had ended. That night in the kitchen Teresa wrote in her journal.

July 31, 1891 ~ It is strange to think of myself as an heiress. It hasn't changed my life yet. But I have made plans. Oh what plans! First is the sale of the ranch in Mexico. This commission is a test of the resolutions Jack made before he left—namely his declaration of love for me and his plan for self-improvement. Next I'll buy a small ranch not far from Tucson and install Jack as foreman. Second, he must swear to be faithful to me & not take up with other women.

I do so miss Jessie. Her company at night, her reading to me—oh, I sometimes wearied of it, but now I would enjoy hearing her read a page of Dickens. Her books sit on the shelf just the way she left them. The only thing I have done is to take out her bed. Federico can now sleep without his little brothers tumbling over him. Oh, I also put her chair in the corner where her bed was.

I must have someone patch the holes where the curtain rods were and calcimine them. And the roof must be replaced. That flood! That terrible time. Yet, it strikes me that the flood which took Jessie also made me a stronger person. Life is so strange at times.

20 La Fiesta de San Agustín ❖ September 2

Tucsonans had been celebrating La Fiesta de San Agustín for three days, but so far Jack had not appeared. Half-heartedly arranging ladies' gloves in the glass display case, Teresa sat on a stool while she kept an eye on two of Chloe's black kittens tussling in a basket in the store window. Luis had allowed her to place them there as long as she cleaned up after them. Manuela had taken the calico, and a customer had already adopted another. The doorbell tinkled as Jack opened it, and her heart seemed to fly up to her mouth.

"Hello, Teresa," he called out, laughing. "See you are now stocking cats at the Emporium."

"Want a kitten? They're free."

"I'm not in the market just now, unless her name is Teresita."

Unshaven, his clothes dirty, Jack strode in with a saddlebag draped over his arm. If he had made a profitable side deal or won at gambling, Teresa surmised he didn't spend money on himself. Though disheveled, his air of confidence seemed intact.

He dropped the saddlebag on the counter and grinned at her as he pulled some bulky papers from it and slapped them down on the countertop. "I wanted you to see these before I take them to Heney. The bill of sale for the Harrington ranch and a bank draft for the earnest money."

"You've done well, Jack."

His blue eyes sparkled under his thick brows as he fingered his mustache. He reached across the counter to take one of Teresa's hands. "Yep, I got 'er done. Teresa, soon as I clean up, let's celebrate. Let's kick up our heels tonight."

"That would be fine. I'd like that."

"Well then, I'll stop by for you at seven. First we'll take in a little of the fiesta and then have supper at the San Xavier. That's where I'm bunking."

"The San Xavier? That place charges three dollars a day!" Teresa raised an eyebrow, her doubts about his promise to reform ready to surface.

"Yes, I've got a fancy room on the top floor," Jack said easily. "With the fiesta going on, it's about the only hotel room left in town. Even boarding houses are full."

"Of course, the town is bursting with people. We'll be ready at seven then."

"We?" Jack echoed. "Who else is coming?"

"Jack, I can't go about town with you without a chaperon. Tía Socorro will be coming too." Teresa thought of the picnic. Why was she so willing to defy convention then and not now? That day in the bosque was pure desperation, she concluded. Now, everything must be proper.

"Teresa! Teresa! You surprise the hell out of me every time you open that pretty mouth. You risk your neck riding south, shoot a man, and single-handedly rescue him in a gully-washing rain. Now you can't walk on Tucson streets and have supper with this same hombre?"

"People in Tucson are well aware that I ride about unescorted on a Sunday. They are used to that. But I don't parade down the streets of this town with a man, nor dine at a hotel with him desacompaña."

"I give up. Bring your aunt along then." Still holding Teresa's hand, he rounded the counter and gave her a quick kiss on the cheek. Stuffing the papers back in the saddlebag, he was out the door, the bell jingling as it slammed.

In her bedroom Teresa stood before the mirror on Jessie's wardrobe door, holding her new gown in front of her. Since she was still in mourning, it was of black silk faille. Draped pleats on the side accented the bustle, and the bodice neck was inset with lace ruching. Earlier that month Teresa had brought the fabric home from the store along with one of the latest patterns from the East, and Socorro had stitched it together.

The turquoise stone on a black band at her throat was the only bright splash of color in her ensemble. Yes, as Socorro suggested, the stone complimented her green eyes. As she hummed a tune, she laid out her undergarments, new silk stockings and kid boots along with a buttonhook. Next she heated water on the stove, dragged the tin bathtub from the washhouse to her kitchen and bathed.

After dressing, she brushed her hair, frowning at the sight of a few gray strands in her dark hair as she pulled it back, twisted it into a knot, and began to pin it up. Then, remembering Luis's compliment about wearing her hair down in the ramada, she parted and rolled up the sides, letting the back fall loose. Why must she turn old before she had tasted the joys of youth? Standing before the mirror again, with a hand mirror she looked at her profile from the side, her hand going to her jaw, as though she might remold it and make it less prominent. But the overall effect of her new hairstyle pleased her. She lifted her chin and squared her shoulders.

From a satin-lined glove box she drew out a pair of black gloves—the box and gloves both new—and pulled them on. Her hairbrush and a black lace handkerchief went into her black-beaded reticule. She smiled at her reflection in the looking glass, a mere new-moon smile at first. But as uncontrollable effervescence arose like bubbles in a mountain spring, she laughed aloud. It seemed like music of the soul to her. She swished her skirt and danced a little jig. At last she had someone to share her life; the disappointed girl still abiding within her was about to receive her due.

21 *The Ring* ❖ *September 2*

Jack sat on the bed in his room polishing his boots. He was tuckered out—he had hit the trail before dawn to get into Tucson by midday. But now he was rarin' to go. His dream was just a ways down the trail. He had a woman he'd taken a shine to and a ring to put on her finger. That ranch he'd been hankering for would be coming to him soon.

"I guess I'm stuck on this Tucson gal. First time in my life it's ever happened. And now I'm just about ready to brand her," he said to himself. Things were not going exactly according to plan. He had meant to soften her up with a little wine and a good supper in their hotel room, then haul out the ring he had in his pocket and ask for her hand. Of course, he would tell her he loved her. That part would be easy because he had decided that what he held in his heart for that tall, stubborn, square-jawed woman was love, if that's what you call this spooked feeling that haunted him most of the time.

He couldn't fail to win her. He'd sold the ranch for the asking price and had hightailed it home to her with the contract. She'd already received a check from Ned's bank, and the income from his ranch would follow in installments, the final payment to be made in five years.

Still, he was a little uneasy about this getting hitched. It was like hobbling a horse that's used to roaming. But he guessed he was about ready to settle down. He worried about her seeing him as just another fortune hunter. Well, how much had her fortune been the bait? By the terms of the contract Ned set up with the lawyer, Jack would have earned a fee of fifteen hundred dollars if he found his daughter within ten years. If he failed to find her in that time, he would get the whole bequest of twenty-two thousand dollars, plus the property. That sure would have been the mother lode all right.

Right off, though, he figured ten years was too damn long to wait for that ranch he dreamed of. Marrying the heiress, if she was single—when and if he found her—had always been part of his plan. He was surprised when it turned out to be Teresa—he'd crossed her off his list long ago. What he hadn't expected was her roping him in. The money was part of it, but it damn sure wasn't all. Having Teresa was frosting on the cake. Ned's daughter! Come to think of it, why hadn't he noticed that she had those green eyes of his, his height, and even his sturdy build?

Jack set down one boot on the carpet and started polishing the other, mouthing the words he wanted to toss off when he proposed to Teresa. This fancy room should have been where he rassled her down and got the stamping iron on her. The perfect place—a walnut dresser, marble-topped table with carved chairs, horsehair couch and an ample bed. But Teresa had spooked on him. Now it had to be in a public place with an old aunt horning in. ¡Esa mosca! Hell, no one could pull the wool over that old cob's eyes for sure. It wasn't supposed to be this way, damn it.

The worst of his problems was the way he'd come by the engagement ring he had in his pocket. Breaking his promise to Teresa, he'd been playing cards all along. Before he ever started out for Mexico he had planned to double, maybe triple that money Ned had left him for finding his daughter. But luck had been against him in one gambling hall after another on Congress Street. And that fifteen hundred dollars had vanished like a desert mirage when you rode up on it. The hell of it was he'd confessed everything to her before he left; flat broke as he was, he had to. She had been as pissed as a wet hen, and he had promised he'd gamble no more.

He meant to stick to that—at least any gambling she'd hear about. Oh well, it wasn't the first time he'd lost a bundle at cards and it damned sure wouldn't be the last. Gambling was in his blood. Down in Sonora at a Magdalena bar Jack had seen a tiger poster advertising faro. He fancied himself an expert at "bucking the tiger." For a while he played faro with a small stake—the traveling money Teresa had given him. His luck went back and forth, his opponents nearly cleaning him out at one point. But he eventually won enough money to get him back to Tucson and then some. He was going to quit then, but he got sucked into a damn poker game.

Winning, losing, winning, losing—on into the night. Had to stay in to get something back. About dawn he wore the other players down. They didn't exactly dance with joy when he raked in the stack of silver pesos and the ring and pulled out of the game. That one time he damn sure knew when to quit. Wanting that ring so bad had been the hook. Trouble was, he wasn't too sure he'd fool Teresa about how he'd come by it.

With a groan Jack pulled on his boots and then slipped a square of blue satin from his shirt pocket. He unwrapped the ring, a square-cut emerald set in a wide band of gold. Unusual hunk of stone, he thought, holding it up to the light. The hombre who once owned it had long slim fingers and Jack was sure it would fit Teresa. But she'd wonder how he came by it. He could say he bought it, but how the devil could he buy such an expensive ring with no money of his own? Could he say he found it? No, Teresa would certainly not believe that. Dang, he had it! He'd say Ned bought it for one of his lady friends, and then they had a falling out. That story would have to do. Teresa was as smart as a whip, so he'd have to make sure that it sounded like the honest-to-God truth. Well, by damn, he's the man who could do 'er.

He folded the ring in its square of satin cloth and placed it back in his shirt pocket. The satin had come from a sweet señorita's sewing basket—that visit to a blue lady another broken promise. In his new story the ring was wrapped in it when he found it in Ned's desk.

Now he had to sell this tale to not one—but two—of those Velarde women. Hell, he was sure glad he had enough money left to pay the hotel bill and this fancy feed, he thought. He had a weakness for women, but always getting a handout from one wasn't in his book.

22 *San Xavier Hotel* ❖ *September 2*

Manuela, giggling, waltzed into Socorro's bedroom where Teresa was dressing her aunt's hair. "Tía Teresa, su amigo está aquí," she said with a grin.

"Gracias, Manuelita, you tease." Teresa gave her a hug. Boys had begun to notice Manuela with her dark eyes and her father's curly hair. "Tía Socorro and I are ready to take in the fiesta."

Chatting amiably with Luis in the parlor, Jack was dressed in a worn brown suit, vest, and a slightly stained hat. Teresa was relieved to see he hadn't been wildly spending money on himself. With a smile and a bow he helped the ladies into the horse and pole buggy he'd hired. Teresa appreciated his stylish dash, and even Socorro responded to it with a pleasant smile. Streets were thick with people celebrating the holiday, and like them, Teresa felt lighthearted and happy.

During the year Tucsonans observed several saints' days, and the largest of these celebrations, La Fiesta de San Agustín, now lasted three weeks. Having outgrown other sites—the Plaza de la Mesilla, the Courthouse Plaza, and Levin's Park—it was now centered in Carrillo's Gardens. As in former years, it began with a high mass and a procession around the church at Plaza de la Mesilla. But the church fathers, while still observing the religious aspect of the saint's day, were no longer involved in the secular festivities because of the violence they spawned.

Now in its fifth day, the fiesta had gained momentum, an alcoholic tide of noise, dust, color, and confusion. Cowpunchers, farmers, miners, wood sellers, and drifters rubbed elbows with Tucson's citizens. Papago and Yaqui vendors sold tortillas, nopalitos, pitayas, pinolé, squash, beans, acorns, medicinal herbs, mescal, and teswin. Displayed at booths or on blankets, ollas, baskets, carvings, guitars, violins, and harps were for sale.

Crouching around the central pavilion, Papago Indians played homemade fiddles and drums. Partners squared up on the pavilion's wooden floor to dance the quadrille, polka, or schottische to the lively music. Teresa was relieved that Jack didn't ask her to dance, a skill she had never acquired, though Mercedes had tried to teach her. When did a bookkeeper ever have a chance to dance?

"Esperenme, que ahorita vuelvo," Jack said, "I'll be right back." He seated Teresa and Socorro at one of the many plank-and-saw-horse tables under the trees. With a fat cigar hanging from his mouth, he soon returned with a tumbler of lemonade in each hand. Teresa smiled as she accepted the drink. "Looks like our new laws are in force this year," she observed. "I don't see any gambling going on."

In previous years staid Tucsonans who otherwise never gambled—women as well as men—had played at tables set up for monte, faro, rouge et noir, and dice. But eventually civic leaders realized that gambling attracted the lawless element that brought violence to the fiesta and had recently enacted laws to prohibit it.

"Sí, but Luis tells me that there are plenty of games this year for those who know where to find them," Socorro said.

Jack innocently lifted his bushy eyebrows. "Oh, is that so? Well now, would you ladies care to take in a rooster pull with me tomorrow?"

"Watch a poor rooster buried in sand up to his neck get his head pulled off? No thank you!" Teresa replied. Socorro agreed with her.

"Those riders have to be real good to stay aboard their cayuses, leaning so far over on their pass. It's a neat trick. Besides, sometimes they pull up the whole bird."

"It's still cruel," Teresa said.

"Then, how about carreras de caballos?" Jack crushed out his cigar in the dirt. "There's a race tomorrow."

"Alas, no horse racing for me. I must work," Teresa said.

"I must also help. Mobs of people in town," Socorro added.

After they finished their drinks, they pushed through the crowd to watch the Yaqui deer dance. The Indians had come from the Rio Yaqui area in Sonora. Singers and dancers gathered under another ramada covered with sycamore branches that was used only for deer dances. Three men sat cross-legged on the edge of the structure, their broad-brimmed hats tipped over their faces as they played instruments and sang—their voices ranging from deep tones to shrill falsetto. Two ran rasping sticks against hollow gourds; the other beat a cornhusk-wrapped drumstick against a drum formed from half of a large gourd.

The barefoot dancer with deer horns tied to his head shook the dry gourds he carried, dipping and winding in a complicated shuffle. Gourd rattles around his waist and ankles lent rhythmic percussion to his steps. Sometimes he stopped to raise his head, testing the wind for scent of his enemies, as a deer would. Teresa tapped her foot to the beat. Though she had seen deer dancers before, she was captured anew by the solemn beauty of the sacred dance.

She saw Lito on the other side of the ramada, nodding his head to the rhythm. When he looked up, he smiled at her, but as his eyes moved on to Jack his smile faded, replaced by a frown. Teresa elbowed her way around the crowd to greet him, but didn't ask him the question that haunted her. When they were alone she'd ask him why he didn't like Jack.

Jack reined in the horse at the San Xavier Hotel at the end of Pennington where it met the railroad tracks. Formerly named Porter's Hotel, the two-story building had been erected for passengers of the Southern Pacific Railroad. He had heard that Tucson's bigwigs sat at the hotel's bar with cigars and brandy to shake hands on business deals.

In keeping with the spirit of the fiesta, the hotel's broad verandas were awash with the glow of Chinese lanterns. Jack smiled with pleasure as he helped the two women from the buggy and tipped the attendant who drove it away. Tonight was a red-letter occasion for him.

"The dining room's not crowded," Teresa said. "I suppose most people are eating at the fiesta's booths. Look, Tía Socorro, white linen table cloths and white candles."

"Yes, and real crystal!" her aunt observed. "I've never seen such splendid table settings. Muy elegante."

The maître d' led them to a table, pulled out a chair for Socorro, and distributed menus. Jack seated Teresa. Without glancing at the menu, he smiled expansively and stroked his mustache. "Bring us some of your best red wine." Belatedly he added, "Ladies, do you like red wine?"

Both women nodded. "Sí."

"I'll have a whiskey. And some oysters would go good," Jack added. Damn, he knew how to order at a restaurant, even if he didn't know how to read.

"They are fresh. Just in from Guaymas today," the waiter recited.

"And what is the specialty of the house?" Jack asked.

"Roast pork with applesauce."

"Does that suit you ladies?" Jack asked.

Socorro and Teresa agreed to his choice.

"Make that three orders of pork."

"Any vegetable?" the waiter continued. "Sweet corn, buttered beets, American peas?"

"Si, si, señor," Socorro said.

"All of them, señora?"

"All of 'em," Jack interjected. "If the lady wants all of 'em, bring her all of 'em."

"And I'll have the sweet corn only," Teresa said.

When their meal was finished, they chose jelly layer cake for dessert with coffee—chocolate for Socorro. Emptying her cup, she dabbed her mouth with her napkin and rose from her chair. "Muchas gracias, Señor O'Brien, estuvo muy sabrosa esta cena. I believe I saw a copy of *El Fronterizo* in the lobby I'd like to read. I'll wait for you there. You enjoy your coffee."

After she left, Jack said, "She's sure a savvy lady. If she saw the name of that paper as we passed by, she got the eyesight of an eagle."

"She's most understanding."

Jack thought uneasily, I'm alone in the corral with Teresa, ready to throw the reata. What if I miss? He pulled a cigar from his coat pocket. "My dear, do you mind if I smoke?"

"No, está bien. Tell me about your trip to Magdalena, Jack."

The smile that lit up her eyes gave him courage. "Everything went off without a hitch. The buyer was rarin' to go, to close the deal. Ranch was in tiptop shape. Oh, did I tell you about that trust fund Ned set up for running it? After the ranch sold, what was left of the fund was to go to Manuel Ortega, the foreman. Smart plan of Ned's. Ortega had to walk a tightrope. Had to figure out just how much to put out for keeping up the ranch, and still not squander his own nest egg."

"That was explained in the will."

"Forgot about that." Watch your step, hombre, this lady knows the ropes, Jack thought.

"Tell me about Eduardo—my father. It's hard to think of him that way. I feel I'm betraying Hector, the man I grew up with."

"He's still your Papá. He raised you up, didn't he?"

"Yes. He used to sing to me, tell me stories, take me for rides. He was a good father—" She broke off while the waiter poured more coffee. "He was a good man before he took to drink. Jack, please tell me about Eduardo—Ned, I guess you call him."

"Ned? Except for that time he, uh, that time with your mother, fue hombre sagaz y honesto. He loved her, y sufria duras penas for what he did to her."

"What he did to my mother was unforgivable."

"He knew that. Triste hombre, he never forgave himself. That's why I was looking for you. He'd say, 'Tengo que pagar la deuda.' That debt wore him down more than the disease, I reckon."

"What was he like?"

"He was fair and honest in his dealings. A real good man."

"Do you know anything about his family?" Teresa asked.

"His mother was Spanish and his father was an English doctor. Creo que Eduardo fue educado en Guadalajara."

"I suppose you learned Spanish from him. I wondered why you spoke the language so well. With such a different accent, unlike nosotros sonorenses."

"Yes, I learned the lingo from Ned." Jack puffed on his cigar for a moment. "A terrible thing happened to Ned and his family. They was attacked by bandits led by an hombre called El Tigre Montes, the Mountain Lion. A bandit. He killed the parents and took Ned captive. His band robbed and murdered all over Sonora. Somewheres around Cocóspera, I think it was, Ned escaped and just kept on going north over the border."

"How old was he then?"

"When he escaped? Nineteen or twenty. We didn't meet until

fifty-four. Well, you know, the year you were born. In age, Ned had nine years on me."

"What did he die from?"

"A tumor in his insides. He just wasted away." Jack shook his head. "Poor hombre had a lot of pain. Damn, it was sure terrible to watch."

"I wish I could have known him. Perhaps if Jessie had married him, things would have been different for her. It's strange to know that I am this man's daughter. It's hard to grasp. It changes my whole life."

"Life does change. You know it's like a river, and we just got to learn to flow with the current." Jack blew a ring of smoke up in the air. Things are going just fine, he decided. He looked into her eyes, now sparkling with tears.

At that moment the waiter sidled up to refill their coffee cups again. Hell, Jack thought, I've lost my opening about changing our lives. Damn that waiter. He took a sip of coffee. "Say, I just thought of something. I bet I know where you got those green eyes of a cat. Ojos de gato. Ned had green eyes like his mother. She came from Northern Spain. Ned was proud of that."

Well, here goes, he thought. "Teresita, I have something to go with those green eyes of yours." He pulled the satin cloth from his vest pocket and unfolded it. The emerald ring sparkled in the candlelight. He took her left hand.

Teresa quickly withdrew it. "Jack. This is not the way." She hesitated for a moment. "Tienes que hablar con Luis. And then the proposal and the ring."

He could scarcely believe this sudden change in her; she was sidestepping and her ears were back. In panic he decided to make his move. "You don't really mean that I got to go and ask Luis, do you? Teresa, I love you. Will you be my wife?"

"Jack, as I said before, you must consult Luis. Esto se tiene que hacer correctamente."

"¿Correctamente, Teresa? This minute you decide to get proper? You know that picnic wasn't exactly proper. At our age why must we follow some silly old rules of courting?" Those green eyes grew cold. They seemed to drill holes in him. He shouldn't have mentioned the picnic.

"It's not only a matter of following social conventions. This is happening much too fast. I have questions I must ask."

"Then ask 'em."

"Where did you get this ring?" Her eyes were still unwavering.

"I found it in Ned's desk," he said looking down at the ring in his hand.

"On this trip and not before when he died? How convenient."

His story about the ring had fallen flat. "Hell! Teresa, do you want to marry me or not? What does it matter how I got the damn ring?"

"Jack, don't curse all the time. I just asked where you got it. That's a simple question. Don't you see, I must be able to trust you? Remember the two promises you made to me? About other women and gambling? How can I trust you if you play me false at the outset?"

He stood up and pocketed the ring. "So I won it in cards! By my skill. I'm a card player and a damn good one. Just you remember that. Jack O'Brien, that's who I am. I was willing to settle down with one woman. Damn if it'll be you. You're sure the hell not going to make me into some lily-livered yes-man."

Heads turned at tables where a few diners still lingered over coffee. Jack strode out of the restaurant. Goddamn woman! Gonna go out and gamble all night long if I have a mind to, he mumbled. He went to the rig and started back to the livery stable to return it. Then he remembered that Teresa and her aunt would be afoot if he took the buggy. He turned around and stomped back into the hotel, finding Teresa, white-faced, sitting next to aunt in the lobby.

"Take the damned buggy. I'll leave it at the door. You haven't got the sense God gave a horsefly, but you sure the hell can drive a buggy."

23 Frank Heney ❖ September

Just past noontime Teresa walked up Meyer Street, on her way to the bank and the library. Her eyes cast down, she scuffed through the dirt as she counted the short shadows of canales projecting from the adobe walls overhead. Enveloped in misery, she relived the scene of that night at the hotel with Jack, as she often had in the past nine days.

Why did she stubbornly try to reform him? Perhaps it's impossible for a man of his age to change. What if he liked the ladies? That was normal. And what if he liked to gamble? Most men in Tucson enjoyed a game of cards. Her own stepbrother did. But in moderation. Luis never endangered his livelihood with a throw of dice. Jack did. He confessed that he had wasted that fifteen hundred dollars before he went to Mexico. But this time he tried to deceive her about the ring. She'd be a fool to marry a man who couldn't be honest with her. Yet, her heart ached for Jack. If he proposed marriage again, she would be hard pressed to refuse him. For how many years had she hoped to become a bride?

July 18, 1878 ~ Mary Scott and Dr. Handy married last night. Everyone has been talking about the wedding for weeks. How I wish I could have gone, but I didn't know her that well at St. Joseph's. Such a pretty girl with her fair hair. Mercedes knows the seamstress who made her wedding dress. It had ruffles with yards of lace & long full sleeves & a long train. The wedding was in the Page's backyard. Heard it was decorated & lit up with candles. Mary must be about the same age as Margarita. I was my sister's maid of honor. All these weddings. Am I never to have one?

A buggy roared by Teresa, the wheels spinning dirt in her face. She looked up in time to glimpse the driver. Dr. Handy, his face twisted in fury, leaned forward to lash his horse, then veered right, directly toward a man crossing the street. Leaping out of the path of the black buggy, the pedestrian hurtled against a building and fell. Teresa rushed toward him, as the buggy rolled on. It happened in mere seconds. "Mr. Heney! Are you all right?"

The slightly-built man bent down, picked up his hat and brushed it off. Teresa handed him his unbroken glasses from the dirt. "Yes, I think so, Miss Velarde." A small crowd gathered around him, some babbling in sympathy, others asking what had happened.

"Where are you going? Let me accompany you," Teresa offered.

Heney looked at her with a smile. "I'm on my way back to court."

"And I'm going to the library."

"Very well, since we're going in the same direction, let me accompany you." The mild-mannered lawyer took Teresa's arm as they crossed Congress Street. "Dr. Handy deliberately tried to run you down. He could have killed you!" she exclaimed. "You can count on me if you need a witness. I can scarcely believe what he just did. He could have killed you."

"That was his intent." Heney patted his right pocket. "At my brother's suggestion, I carry a gun now. Doesn't do much good when Handy tries to run me down with his buggy. Ever since I agreed to represent his wife, he's behaved like a madman. He's still attempting to gain title of their Stone Avenue home for his mother."

Everyone around town had heard of Dr. Handy's threats to kill the man who defended his wife, first in their divorce and then in the eviction suit currently being heard in Superior Court. Townspeople knew of his affair with another woman and that he continued to prescribe morphine for his wife. She confided to friends that he often chained her to a bedpost when he was away from home.

"I wondered why you took Mary Handy's case in the first place. Considering all the threats he's made to kill you, it was very brave of you."

"Miss Velarde, I would have to take down my shingle if anyone could bully me into refusing to take a case I believed in. However, I don't usually risk incurring Handy's wrath when I'm alone. As a rule, I have someone walk around town with me. Foolishly, I took a chance today."

◆ ◆ ◆

John Handy tried to best Frank Heney later that month. By following newspaper accounts and listening to the stories bruited about town, Teresa learned of the tragic confrontation between the two men. At noon on September 24, the doctor attacked the lawyer near the corner of Pennington and Church Streets. In the scuffle for possession of Heney's gun, Handy was shot. The bullet, lodged in his abdomen, had to be removed. Other doctors were on hand, but Handy insisted that they summon Dr. George E. Goodfellow, a Tombstone surgeon skilled in gunshot wounds, to perform the operation. Hours later, a special Southern Pacific engine carried Goodfellow to Tucson. The surgeon operated, but at midnight Handy died. Heney surrendered to authorities, but most Tucsonans, aware of the doctor's threats, believed he had acted in self-defense.

Two days later Dr. Handy's body lay for public viewing at the Masonic Hall on the second floor of the Cosmopolitan Hotel. Teresa climbed the stairway and from the doorway looked into the room filled with throngs of mourners—most dressed in black. Some knelt before the wooden coffin placed on a bier near the window. Dozens of candles flickered on the table behind it, and masses of flowers scented the hot, airless room. Murmured prayers of mourners floated upward with the smoke.

It seemed to Teresa that half the town had come to honor the highly esteemed doctor. She was hardly surprised. This was the man who had treated Apaches and earned their respect. He had offered his services to the county's poor at nominal cost, and had given free vaccinations during the smallpox epidemic several years ago. Teresa would never forget how he cared for her mother with skill and compassion. Her sympathy lay primarily with his wife—Mary Handy had suffered from his abuse and was said to be quite ill now. Yet Teresa was saddened by the tragic death of this man with the uncontrollable temper, the Tucson physician who had had no equal.

Someone joined her at the doorway. It was Jack. Their eyes met, but neither spoke. Teresa reacted to his presence as she did the first time he walked into the Emporium. Dizzy, her breath suspended, she feared her legs would not support her. She longed to collapse against his broad chest, to feel his arms around her. Alarmed that her overpowering desire must be apparent to him, she fled, almost stumbling down the stairs. Outside, she leaned against the wall to slow her breathing and collect herself before returning to the Emporium.

September 30, 1891 ~ Read in the paper that a few Apaches attended Dr. Handy's funeral. Not just our tame Apaches, but from the reservation. I still fear them, but I suppose they are like any people, some good & some bad. If driven to desperation, they become wild & murderous.
    My life is wretched. I cry so easily & am short with everyone. Mercedes talks with me & that helps. Though sometimes I want only to be let alone.

Teresa combated her misery by plunging into work at the Emporium. She also searched through newspaper advertisements for a small ranch. Her determination to buy one had not abated, although she would need to find someone other than Jack to help her run it. When he went to Mexico for her in August, he had given up his job at Dos Colinas. She learned from Luis that he had found another job at a ranch in Canyon del Oro. Except for those few moments at the Masonic Hall, she had not seen him. But when she walked around town, she glanced down every cross street and scrutinized every horseback rider and passing wagon. In her mind's eye she could see his face, his beetle brows, his blue eyes glinting at her, his silvery blonde mustache.

24 A Cup of Champurro ❖ October 17

To prepare for the day when she would leave the store, Teresa started training Manuela to keep the Emporium's books. The plan met with Luis's approval, and Manuela was proving to be an apt apprentice. Originally Olivia objected, not wanting to be robbed of a nursemaid, housemaid, and cook. But that problem was solved by Tía Socorro. She had returned to Mexico after the fiesta, but she wrote to Teresa and Luis, announcing her decision to move to Tucson for good. She would be delighted to help Olivia with her brood.

Teresa and Lito had already made several trips scouting for a ranch in the desert around Tucson, when an advertisement for a small ranch along the Rillito River and Pantano Wash appeared in the newspaper. She decided to take a look at this property.

On a cold October morning, Teresa and Lito headed up Stone Avenue in the Verlarde wagon, following a mule-drawn streetcar part of the way. In the decade since the arrival of the railroad, Tucson had put on certain Eastern airs. They passed homes, not of adobe, but of wood, with porches decorated with grillwork and cornices. Fenced front yards adorned with trees and flowers were a new concept to Teresa. She liked their look of refinement.

A mile east of town they passed the new School of Mines, a gracious, two-story building. The land-grant university, which had opened the previous month, was primarily a mining and agricultural school, though it boasted of liberal arts courses as well. Teresa promised herself she would enroll one day.

As their horse jogged along, Teresa watched the cloud shadows on the Santa Catalinas, the closest of the four mountain ranges that surrounded the valley where Tucson lay. As a child growing up in their awesome presence, her gaze had always been drawn to them, a

lodestar where north lay. Seemingly immutable in form, the towering peaks and deep valleys defied their immutability, changing season
after season and moment by moment. As the sun inched west and
cloud shadows played across them, light shifted like a kaleidoscope of
rose, mauve, lavender, blue, and dark purple. She had also known the
Catalinas more intimately. The distant blue peaks seen from her home
seemed to bear little kinship to the rugged, boulder-strewn canyons
she had climbed through on hunting trips with Luis and Lito.

Lito turned east, heading toward the Rincon Mountains. They
passed Fort Lowell. Abandoned for months, it had taken on the sad
look of a desert derelict. The wooden doors and window frames of
the adobe buildings that had not been sold at public auction had been
appropriated. Teresa noticed that the Mexican families who now
lived in the buildings covered their doors and windows with rugs or
hides. Brown-eyed children stood in front of one of the homes, shyly
staring at them as they drove by.

"Look, sartas de chiles colorados." Teresa pointed to the long
strings of bright red chili peppers that hung against the walls of most
dwellings. "Lots of work—roasting and grinding them into chili
powder."

"Sí, it takes time, but all the cooking we used to do took time.
Grinding the corn took María hours. And when that was scarce, she
ground up péchita, mesquite beans, instead. And we hung slices of
beef on mesquites to dry and covered it with cheesecloth to keep off
the flies."

"I remember that. . . Oh, Lito, there's Corbett Ditch. Stop there,
por favor. I want to pick some berro, watercress. It will please Socorro. And we may as well picnic here."

Corbett Ditch, lined with towering cottonwood and ash trees,
irrigated rich farmland. Corn, squash and melons grew in the fields.
A dense mesquite bosque, its bare black trunks twisted in a winter
dance, lined the Rillito River, a watercourse born at the confluence of
the Pantano and Tanque Verde Washes.

After Teresa gathered watercress, she and Lito sat on the wagon
bench to eat beans wrapped in tortillas and sip water from a canteen.
They ate in silence, Teresa preoccupied, longing for what might have
been. Sometimes she cast Jack as an unregenerate villain, but most

often she blamed herself for the failed romance, for her folly in being too rigid. She wanted to talk about it to Lito, but hardly knew how to begin.

"I watched the deer dance at the fiesta with my friend, Jack O'Brien. I saw you across the way and noticed you had a very stern look on your face when you looked at him."

"Ah, mi amiga, at last you speak of the heart."

"The heart? What do you mean?"

"I see the long face and the sad breath you have. You have not obeyed your heart."

"If you mean about Jack—well, there are reasons why I didn't. But I was certain then, Lito, that you did not approve of him. That's why I am asking about it."

"That was then. Now I know another thing. What you have become is not good."

"What have I become?"

"I have said, a woman with a long face and sad breath. You should be with this man."

"With Jack? Are you saying that I should take up with him again?"

"Sí."

"You know he is a jugador, a gambler."

"Sí, lo se."

"I doubt that I could change him."

"Sí, sé eso tambien."

Teresa turned to the old Indian in consternation. "Then do you mean I should marry him anyway? Knowing I can't change him?"

"You can change the way *you* think about him, about card playing, no?"

"Yes, I suppose I could try."

"Playing cards is not such a bad thing. He may have goodness in other ways to make up for that. Do what your heart bids you. Your unhappy heart makes you sick in the soul."

Teresa looked at Lito again, wonder on her face. He shook the carthorse's reins and drove on. She heard the call of a quail off in the desert—a sound like wild, eccentric laughter. She smiled, then laughed, and Lito laughed with her.

The agent who was showing the property took Teresa and Lito

inside the adobe ranch house. It was crumbling and would have to be replaced, she thought, remembering the wooden houses in town she had admired. They next toured the outbuildings, a new barn and bunkhouse. The corral fencing was in good shape. A windmill drew water for the house, garden, and stock tank. After they left the agent, Lito drove Teresa around the property in the wagon. The ranch nestling against the Rincon Mountains was covered with creosote bushes, palo verdes, mesquite, and a file of saguaros marched across it. The spread proved to be what Teresa hoped for. She would buy it, and name it Rancho Velarde. She knew exactly who she would ask to run it with her.

Leaning over the casa grande's dining room table, Teresa was cutting out a new dress for Socorro, whose short stature made it hard for her to do it. It had been a week since the wagon trip with Lito, and Teresa had yet to screw up the courage to contact Jack. She hoped she'd run into him in town, but she still hadn't seen him.

"Sometimes I think I'll take Lito's advice about Jack, and at other times I simply don't know," Teresa said. "Jack hasn't been knocking down my door. I don't know that he cares for me anymore."

"No one can advise you in this, this affair of the heart," Socorro said, taking pins from her mouth as she basted skirt panels together at the other end of the table.

"Lo se bien. So many nights I've lain awake fretting. I can't concentrate on anything. It's a good thing Manuela has begun to work for her papá. Soy inútil, useless. No sirvo para nada."

Socorro put down the fabric she was basting and took the scissors from Teresa. "Come, Palomita, let's have a cup of my hot champurro."

Teresa smiled. "Tía Socorro, you believe that a cup of hot chocolate will cure anything."

"Maybe not a broken heart. But you can warm it up with my good chocolate."

Luisa and Alejandro were playing on the floor with the last of Chloe's litter, a calico kitten. Manuela had adopted her and given her the name Tomas before she realized the kitten was a female. She became Tomasita.

"¡Chocolate! Chocolate! Tía Socorro, can I have some too?" Alejandro cried.

"Sí, sí, niños," Socorro said, stooping to kiss them both.

"And Federico won't get none," Alejandro said with satisfaction.

" 'Any.' Won't get 'any.' No, he's at school," Teresa said. "Next year you'll be at school too."

In the kitchen Tomasita wound around Teresa's ankles until she poured a saucer of milk for her. Teresa sadly remembered how Jessie made hot chocolate with milk. It was quite different from her aunt's Sonoran champurro that was made with water, cinnamon, raw sugar, and toasted flour to thicken it. When this mixture was heated, Socorro plunked in a few disks of dark chocolate, stirring them with her wooden molinillo until they melted. Warning the boys to let it cool, she set thick earthenware cups of champurro on the table.

They were sipping the hot drink when Olivia appeared in the doorway, an annoyed frown on her face because her siesta had been interrupted. "That Mr. O'Brien is here to see you, Teresa."

Teresa quickly set her cup down on the edge of a plate of Socorro's pan de huevo, golden bread covered with powdered sugar. Spilling chocolate on the table, she picked up a cloth to wipe it up.

"I'll do it, Palomita. Go. ¡Vamos!" Socorro shooed her out the kitchen door.

Jack stood in the parlor, hat in hand. "Señorita Velarde." He paused for a moment, apparently uncertain how to begin. "¿Como está Usted?"

Usually so fluent in Spanish, Teresa thought he seemed to be at a loss for words. He seemed completely lacking in his usual aplomb, and she realized he had also been in turmoil. She said, "Very well."

"Are you very well?" He raised his bushy eyebrows.

"No, Señor—Jack, I've not been—" How could she explain her misery?

"You've not been happy?" he supplied for her.

She shook her head. "No."

"I haven't either. Any chance we could . . . any way we could start again?"

She sat on a petit point chair and gestured to the one beside it, sighing deeply. "Please sit, Jack. Let's talk. There must be a way we can settle our differences."

He put his hat on the marble-topped table near the door and sat down in the parlor. "Yes, I believe we can. First, if a woman expects a man to change the way he is—the way he's always been, she is expecting a heap of changing all at once."

"I think I may be—"

"No, listen. I can't suddenly become another person. But I sure can work at it. My gambling's the hitch. All I can say is if I do get in a poker game, I can try not to play for real high stakes. To hold back some. Don't know if it's possible, but I'll try."

"Oh, Jack, I have been unreasonable. Luis gambles. Lots of people do. It's not just that. I want to be able to trust you. To know that you'll always tell me the truth. To me everything depends on trust and honesty between us."

"Yes, I know I wasn't honest about that ring. I was afraid I would lose you if I told you how I really got it." Jack traced the lavender and rose petit point flowers on the arm of his chair as he talked. "It's funny the way I won it. I was about to clear out, when this Mexican stands up and orders me to play another hand. Orders me with his hand on his holstered pistol! So I do. In the deal I pick up three fours, so I open. The next hombre raises and I stay in. I catch another four on the next draw—"

Teresa laughed.

"I guess you're not much interested in a poker game."

"I wasn't laughing at that. You are running your finger along that rose as if it is one of your lucky cards. I'm sorry. Finish telling me about the game."

"I cleaned him out. His money and that ring. I still have it. You can have it if you want it."

"Do you mean I can just plain have it, or only if I'll marry you? Jack, say what you mean."

"Either way, marry me or not. I got the ring for you. It's yours. But if you think we can get along, you can have both me and the ring. I'd like us to be—I mean. Oh hell— Teresa, will you marry me?" Jack reached across the small table between their chairs and took her hand.

Teresa struggled to keep from breaking out in laughter, laughter born of a fountain of joy welling up in her. "Yes, Jack, I will marry you."

"Well, doggone it! I didn't bring the ring with me. I didn't think—"

"What! No ring?" Teresa laughed again, relieved that she had been given license to laugh, to release the emotion damned up within her. She squeezed his hand playfully. "You cad!"

Jack searched her face for meaning and then chuckled. "I didn't even know I was coming here when I started out today. I've been feeling lower than a snake's belly, fretting on how I ever got hooked on someone so set in her ways. Didn't even know where I was until I saw this house. Just up and knocked on the door, kind of without thinking."

"Jack, I'm glad you came. I'll marry you, ring or no ring."

"I'll bring it soon. Lucky thing I'm in town buying supplies. I'll bring the ring next trip to town, and I'll speak to your brother like you asked."

"That's the proper thing to do. Now, Jack, tell me something. Are you sure you aren't marrying me for my money?" Teresa's eyes sparkled, but the question was more serious than her flippant tone suggested.

Jack stood and walked over to the window looking out. "I've thought about that a good deal. At first I hankered after that money of Ned's something awful. Even before I knew you, it lured me like a streak of color in a rock wall. And after I knew you were the heiress, I still found it mighty attractive—having money, that is."

Jack turned to face Teresa. "But in these last weeks I got clear on things. I had a lot of time to think. Out alone chasing mamma cows a good bit of the time—they're stubborn too, hard to catch. Found out that it was more than the money—I wanted you, plain and simple." He strode back to her chair. "That's how it is with me. Do you believe me?"

"Sí, te lo creo, Jack."

He drew her to her feet, lifted her chin, and held her close to him. "Te amo, Teresa."

"Y yo a tí," she whispered.

"¿Me permites un beso?" he asked softly. He kissed her without waiting for an answer.

Teresa kissed him back, and then with a smile she pushed away to look at him. She was pleased to see the old self-assurance in his eyes and hear it in his voice. Even if it was the confident, swaggering Jack before her, she perceived that he had changed; they had both changed. He possessed a sensitivity he lacked before, and she had seen her own self-assurance blossom since she had known him. Both had discovered new dimensions in their lives. And that, she surmised, must be the essence of love.

"You may kiss me again, mi querido."

Epilogue ❖ Spring 1991

On a Sunday afternoon Rachel Benton sat reading in the rocking chair on Rancho Velarde's wide veranda. For days she had immersed herself in her grandmother's diaries, choosing one to read at random. Then arranging them in chronological order, she started reading them a second time. The handwriting, large and childlike in the first diaries, had become small, spidery, and hard to read in the last. Before she read the final entries, she took off her glasses, glanced up at the Santa Catalina Mountains to rest her eyes, and, she confessed, to postpone reaching the end.

May 25, 1912 ~ My beloved husband passed away on April 29th. He & our son Hector were driving home from Tucson in the buckboard a few weeks ago when he first had this terrible pain in his chest. Dr. Stevenson came out to tend to him, he seemed to be getting better. But then before dawn a few days later the pain returned & he was taken almost instantly. I am so full of grief & sadness. How I wish I had Tía Socorro to comfort me, but she is gone too. She died this very day 4 yrs ago. Went in to Tucson to put flowers on her grave & Jack's today.

October 16, 1912 ~ I still moon about the place too much thinking of my Jack. Life with him was not always smooth—for he had those gambling spells of his and I would make his life miserable for a day or two afterward. But he never gambled with large sums of money as he had promised and somehow we always managed to patch things up. I guess our love or maybe our stubbornness saw us through those hard times. How I wish he was here now. I'd not rail at him for his weakness for cards. Nor his fondness for food. I chided him too much about that big belly of his these last few years.

Manuela has been so good to me since Jack died, though my chief comfort is Jessie Luisa. For her age our daughter is so wise and she knows when to talk and when to be silent. Though I must watch out for her, for she and her father were very close and she is at that tender age—almost but not quite a woman—when things hurt so.

November 21, 1913 ~ Twenty-second Wedding Anniversary. Jack's and mine. I always think of that special day when we were married at the Congregational Church. Luis gave me away, and Manuela was my bridesmaid. Mercedes arranged the flowers. Jack and I honeymooned in San Diego, Calif. What a lovely town on that beautiful ocean.

November 30, 1913 ~ Dear Manuela has blossomed into a lovely wife. My niece was sought after by many young men, but she chose Dr. Walter Stevenson. Manuela wants me to come live in town, but Jessie Luisa and I shall stay here on the ranch, though she stays with Manuela during the week to go to school. And Hector is at a dormitory at the University. He graduates next year as an engineer. Jack would be so proud of his son, that son I bore so late in life. Jack wanted his son to get the education he never had. Luis begged him to work at the store, but Hector went his own way.

    Alas, I never found time to pursue higher education. I guess Jack & this ranch were schooling enough for me. We worked hard day in & day out, me in my garden and with my canning, and Jack with his cattle. From dawn to sundown. Those were sure good years.

January 12, 1914 ~ Mercedes is coming to spend the day with me. Says I shouldn't be alone so much. I got out of the cattle business after Jack passed, tho' I still have a milk cow and two riding horses. I can't keep up the garden anymore. I should hire someone to help me with the place.

    Mercedes gave up her fine sewing, couldn't see well enough anymore. She has time on her hands & has taken to religion. Today she comes here and we'll talk while I piece that quilt for Jessie Luisa.

That was the last entry of Teresa O'Brien's diary. The remaining pages were filled with pencil sketches of her family, the ranch house, cattle, chickens, and her beloved Santa Catalina Mountains.

Rachel closed the last journal and took off her glasses again to wipe the tears from her eyes. She twisted the emerald ring she wore, glancing down at it, thinking that it had almost ended the marriage before it happened.

Her grandmother's presence very much with her, she purposefully gripped the arms of the rocker to stand up. It was high time to fix supper for her family.

CPSIA information can be obtained at www.ICGtesting.com
Printed in the USA
LVOW042233151212

311830LV00004B/850/P